DOG CHRIST

A NOVEL

LUCIAN MORGAN

Copyright © 2020 by Anthony Parella
All rights reserved.

No part of this book may be reproduced in any form or by any electronic or mechanical means, including information storage and retrieval systems, without written permission from the author, except for the use of brief quotations in a book review.

This novel is a work of fiction. Any resemblance by the characters contained herein with persons alive or otherwise is a mere coincidence and an inference made by the reader who is entitled to do so. Except for the dog who is quite real.

Portions of the poem INVICTUS by William Ernest Henley (public domain) quoted with respect and admiration for the author.

Cover painting by Anthony Parella

lucian.morgan@gmail.com

Published in 2020 by Daisy Dog Press, a division of the Sparky the Dog Entertainment Empire

ISBN-13: 978-1467921084

for all the dogs I've ever known

*What crawling villain
preaches abstinence
& wraps himself
in the fat of lambs?*

William Blake *America, a Prophesy*

ONE

THE MAN and the woman live on the side of a mountain in a house built entirely of stone brought by ships from Italy. There are no stones left in Italy because of their house.

It began as a flat spot on the bridge of the mountain's nose, excavated by erstwhile Mayan princes and the sons of pyramid builders. With brown heads wrapped in wet rags against the brutal desert sun, they pounded on the stones for nearly an eon. When winter came they huddled around fires set in rusty drums and rubbed their raw, weary hands until the morning chill broke and they could take up their tools and pound some more. All the while screaming machines with enormous arms that swung and lumbered scraped and scooped and drilled upon everything that makes a house, and the unending procession of growling trucks jammed the narrow road carved into the mountain's cheek expressly for their accommodation, their protestations of a load too great unheeded, unrelieved, their moaning *no more, no more of this,* for the world to hear. So great was the clangor and clang that the human voice was silenced save the bosses' exhortations to carry on. The season passed, the summer's terrible heat returned and the pace of work quickened. Grimy flatbeds roared up the steep mountain trail hauling trees wholly grown while the brown men scratched at the mountain's stony soma for a trace of soil in which to lay the trees' thick roots, and from giant muddy spools, lawn was laid out upon everything that wasn't pool, patio or driveway until at last there stood a house, nearly realized. More trucks followed, less grimy, containing items of furniture and decorative embellishments; other men, less brown, wearing white overalls and blue covers on their shoes placed each item in one of two possible locations, the man and the woman yelling at one another the entire time.

I was there. This is what I remember.

TWO

THEY TAKE their breakfast on the east patio at an enormous glasstop table beneath blue umbrellas. The man casts his keen eye toward the morning vista, as he is most pleased and proud of the view. Visitors are obliged to admire the view and are encouraged to stand as close to the edge of the precipice as possible until they say something like, *damn nice view* or *helluva perch you got here, kids.* By such phrases the man and the woman are roundly gratified. This is what they'll see: the red tile roofs of all the lesser houses below; slivers of pool, patio and driveway amid a forest of wholly grown trees; the thin helix of a road that winds down the canyon and takes the people away and brings them home again; a field of golf; the spire of a church; a village of scant small shops: a grocery, a dry cleaners, a gas station, a favorite restaurant, two casual wear boutiques, a pool supply store; and beyond, a distant line of hazy purple mountains and the listless desert to the horizon; above, a dome of blue and brown.

Even so, the man and the woman prefer to watch teevee while eating their eggs. Their favorite show is the one where the cranky old man and the nervous redhead demonstrate how to be cheerful. Also, coffee is unimaginably important to them. If the coffee is good the woman will say, *Hmm, good coffee this morning,* and the man will turn away from the teevee momentarily to taste his coffee. *Yes, that is good coffee,* he will tell her.

In addition to watching teevee and drinking coffee, the man must talk on the phone as much as is humanly possible. I believe he must be in the phone business. On his little phone he is very instructive. He tells others what to do, how to do it, and who they must do it to. He even tells them what words to use. His favorite thing to say on the phone is goddamnit. This morning his phone conversations require an extra measure of goddamnits owing to an unspecified agitation. He rises grunting from the table and marches round and round the pool, the phone in his non-gesturing hand, firing volleys of goddamnits off the mountain and into outer space.

The woman's job is to get mad when the eggs get cold. It is not possible to prepare an egg to her satisfaction. When the waitress brings the eggs, the woman says, *No good. Tell chef to make new eggs.* She also talks on the phone, although I do not believe she is in the business unless she is in charge of acquisitions. After talking on the phone, earnest young boys or old men in ball caps and sneakers will appear at the gate with the thing she wants. However, she is more than likely to send them away with it. *No good,* she will say. *Bring me a different one.*

This morning she is talking on the phone with the woman she does not like about a party they are planning together. I listen closely as this concerns me. The party is to be held here at the house, and soon. I am not pleased to hear it. Many people will come, a number too great to count. They will dress in fancy costumes and drink too much. The men will shout about money and golf, and at least one woman will have the sort of laugh that can be heard above all others. A band of musicians who once played for them when they were young will play for them again. And then, the big event, an auction for charity, wherein everyone, having brought with them some piece of crap from home, will sell it and buy someone else's piece of crap until all the crap is bought and sold, and by this method the lives of children in Ethiopia will be immeasurably improved. Afterwards they'll dance.

My status here has not been confirmed. The man and the

woman claim to be my parents but I have my doubts. I would demand a DNA test, if I could.

For one thing, not even remotely do I resemble either one of them. The woman, owing to her smallish skull and that tiny nose the man bought for her, bears the simian trace of an australopithecine. Best not to look directly at the nose. Apparently there was this nose in a magazine. Also, my hair is not alternately the color of overripe pomegranates or dead lawn. I have a normal nose and my hair is irrevocably brown, unlike the man who is nearly bald. Out of spite for the remaining hairs he shaves his head every day, clean as a light bulb. I do not shave, although my hand is steady enough most of the time and my beard is grander than any the man could ever hope to grow. Furthermore, I am not short and round like the woman or a lumbering bub like the man about whom everything is large and awkward, and my skin is not the color of pale pink roses but the healthy, sun-kilned hue of a person who works with his hands outdoors. I am not fragile like the woman or angry like the man, nor do I shout and scream or talk on the phone or watch teevee. I am not clumsy or arrogant or rude. I am uncommonly graceful and I am fine.

I remember being four but not fourteen, seven but not seventeen. Today is my birthday. I know this because they sang the song and the woman gave me an unworn shirt. The man gave me a car which made the woman mad because I do not drive cars. She says to him, *What kind of present is that for your only child. It's more like a present for you.*

The man declines to argue. In his reasonable voice he explains that he made a deal for another car, and this car, my birthday car, was thrown in. I'm not sure how it is that a car is thrown in, unfamiliar that I am with the language of business, but I have one now as one was so thrown. I hope the car is English. The mechanic hates the English.

They press me to drink coffee with them, for this is what people should do. The waitress places a full cup directly in front of me.

The woman gasps. In a flash with single swipe of my graceful arm I sweep the cup from the table. It shatters to pieces on the patio stones.

The woman snaps at the waitress. *I thought I told you about this. Never in front of him. Always in the middle so he has to reach,* pounding the proper place on the table with her finger.

Sorry, missus. Forgot, says the girl and scurries to clean up the mess. It seems to me she is new. I don't remember seeing her before. This new waitress is small like a child but not so young, I think. She is quite pale and her hair is as white as a pillowcase. As she stoops to collect the broken shards I would tell her that I regret the mess, that it was a completely reflexive action, like a sneeze, like my speech. Truly, I apologize, I would say. I would also tell her that I do not believe in table service.

The waitress returns to the kitchen to fetch a new beverage for me, milk this time in a preferred plastic cup. She places it correctly on the glass top table just out of my reach. I stretch to retrieve the cup and take a sip. The woman says to the waitress,

Now come, I want you to meet our son. This is Gustav. The girl has a pretty smile. *You may call him Gustav, but not Gus or Gussie. Do you understand?*

The waitress answers, *Yes, ma'am.*

Good, says the woman. *And please remember what we discussed.*

Yes, ma'am, repeats the waitress.

And turning to me the woman says, *This is Anna Marie, our new housekeeper. Anna is from...where is that again, dear?*

*Argent...*the girl tries to tell her.

Anna is from Argentinia, the woman informs me, polysyllabically challenged as she is. *Isn't that interesting?*

No, I reply, which makes the man laugh.

And the woman says, *He means yes. Remember, we talked about this too. He says yes when you ask him a yes question and no when you ask him a no question.*

The waitress replies, *I remember, ma'am.*

The woman pats me on the knee and gives me the smile that means she suffers too.

And Gussie, her husband is going to be our new chef and he's all the way from France. Isn't that interesting?

No, I tell her.

The man chuckles. Instantly she realizes her mistake and tells the girl,

He means yes. The man adds, *You're supposed to say, Gustav, do you think that's interesting?*

Yes, I am obliged to report.

There, like that, he tell the girl. *We have a parrot for a son, but he's harmless and you'll treat him right, I'm sure.*

Yes sir, the girl replies. Her voice is soft and gentle.

Now the man instructs the woman. *Try it again, Lillian. About the cook. Like the doctors told you to.*

The woman gives it another go. *Her husband is the new chef and he's all the way from France. Isn't that....*(harrumph, from the man) *do you think that's interesting?*

Yes, I say.

She receives the nod of approval from the man and carries on. *He's a very famous chef. He used to make lamp chops for the Vice President of the United States, but now he's going to make lamp chops for us.*

All the people in the village eat lamp chops. The village is called Paradise. The woman is called Lilly Deal. The man is called Otto Deal. My full name is Gustav Arturo Deal, after a grandfather who was a German during a war.

I do not live in the stone house. I live in the gardening shack around back, what the woman calls the guest's house. My only piece of furniture is also a lawn mower. The spoons in the drawer are covered in mud from digging in the flowers. I do not receive mail. And I measure time not in years, but in eras, epochs and eons. It is my hope that one day I become a fossil.

At the glasstop table the man sips his coffee and says to me,
 Like your new car, captain?
 Yes, I tell him.

Don't, says Lilly.
Don't what, he replies, knowing full well.
You should get him a decent present, that's all.
Like what? grumbles the man.
Something nice. Something he can use.
He can have anything he wants. All he has to do is ask for it.

This therapy tinged response does not please the woman. *A present is supposed to be something you want that you didn't ask for.*

Otto turns to me. *So whaddya need, boy, eh? Speak up. Just say the words and I'll get you six. I'll get you a hundred.*

Stop it, the woman tells him.

Maybe some pants to go with that pretty shirt. You come up to my closet and we'll pick you out a pair. Have 'em tailored for you. You want some pants? Yes, pants?

Yes, I say.

For christsakes, the woman says, turning away.

He says he wants pants, mommy. Why can't he have pants? Everybody could use a pair of pants.

Something new, Otto. Like a real gift.

I just gave him a sixty-six jag. I think that constitutes a real gift in anybody's book. He's still getting the pants. Right after breakfast, boy.

End of discussion. Lilly is taking it hard. She folds her arms and mumbles, *You're not getting him anything then.*

Goddamnit, mutters Otto. The man is in a mood.

People will often ask what's the matter with me. Otto knows. Otto will tell them. *Boy's gone retarded,* he'll say.

They argue some more about my birthday car, then Lilly calls the waitress over and sends back the eggs.

THREE

Glorious, he yawks. *Glorious!* He proclaims it like a madman. Otto Deal, father.

This as I enter their bathrooms, a bifurcated affair the size of center field. The right is indisputably his, the left unquestionably hers. In my powerful motor chair I steer Ottoward to receive a pair of pants.

The man has sequestered himself inside the toilet, a marbled room inside a marbled room. From within this stony chamber I can hear the vocal exercising of his critical faculties. Something in a magazine has caught his attention and apparently it's glorious. He bellows. *Glorious, laborious, borious...*the man loves to rhyme. He is a poet at the core and cannot be contained. New words spring like weeds in the cracks of his vocabulary.

It's a straight shot past the shower and sink and a hard left at the fancy tub they never use round to the woman's side, a pinky gold version of the man's goldy blue layout, all girled up with silks and frills and a fragrance that very much wants to be flowers. The woman is sitting athwart her morning mirror, vaguely unfamiliar with herself she is and subject to fugitive reflections. She is playing with her little crystal bottles of goo. As I pass she says to me, *Mommy wants you to shave this morning, dear.* Back through the bedroom, the interval from door to door requiring the artful negotiation of their perfect bed, a relic, I am often reminded, hand carved by bedmaking monks long deceased. I re-enter Otto's.

The man is in his shower now. From behind glass block I hear him splashing around like a giddy manatee. He is singing a song of his own invention: *la dee da...do dee do....*

Around again to Lilly. The woman is powdering the nose. I hold up and wait. When she moves on to the hair I proceed. Brushing, blowing, brushing. It is one of the few things she is able to do with the effortless coordination of both hands. I hit the throttle and swing around again.

Otto is now at his sink, berobed in a purple hue, head and face covered with shaving cream. In the mirror he watches the reflection of the teevee hanging on the wall behind him. A man is talking about money and what it might mean. *Boomy, doomy, gloomy,* Otto chimes in as he takes a big swipe with his razor from back of neck to top of head. *How 'bout a quick shave there, captain?* he says to me, brandishing his fuzzy razor. But I am gone.

Lap three.

Lilly emerges from her dressing room and I nearly hit her as I speed in. She has already donned the daily uniform—black slacks with very sharp creases (this the dry cleaners know about all too well), the inner pre-shirt tucked in and the main shirt out and unbuttoned. The shirt tail will cover her significant posterior as modern science has yet to conquer the ass. From her jewelry drawer she selects two identical spangly banglies for my inspection. *This one or this one?* she asks as I whiz by.

I come across Otto in his dressing room talking to his clothes. I stop to listen.

Atten-shun! he commands. *Snap to, everyone. Look alive, you suits. Shoulders back, cuffs out.* He drops his robe to the floor. The Supreme Commander of All Forces is naked. *I want to see my underwear front and center,* he orders and removes from the drawer a pair of perfectly folded briefs. The concentration required to maintain his balance is intense. One false move....He feels very special in his underwear. He could rule the world in his shorts. The sox are next. He barks, *I want two blue volunteers for a dangerous mission in my shoes.* He turns to me and winks. *Let's get you some pants,* he says, but I'm off.

When I swing back the woman is waiting for me, directly in my path. I hit the brakes. *Gustav, get over there and let your father get that beard off your face. You look like a caveman with that thing. Doesn't he look like a caveman, Ot?*

I don't wait for Ot's reply. I get up out of my chair and walk out the door. The woman yells back at me, *Don't leave this chair in here, Gustav. Gustav! Daddy's going to get you a nice present today.*

I hide, and when they leave the room I retrieve my chair. I don't think I'd get very far without it anyway, not today. Down the elevator to the main floor, I pass through the kitchen. The new French chef is at the sink washing the dishes. When he sees me he sticks out a soapy hand which I refuse.

You must be zee son, Gustav. I say nothing.

He talks some more but he's difficult to understand, unfamiliar that I am with foreign languages.

Lotsa good food I make you, eh? My lamp chops, they are manny feek. Maybe you like zem?

I do not know what zem is.

Dis is okay. Ma damn mommy tells me what you eat. Crackers with zee cheese, zee tuna fish sandwich, zee spaghetti in zee can. I make nice for you.

The French chef is a small, hairy man with a touch of Cro-Magnon lingering on a chromosome. Also, there's something strange going on with his neck, like it's somehow locked in place. He moves about like a furry robot. I doubt he is capable of making a simple tuna fish sandwich. When he begins to speak again I leave.

The path to the gardening shack runs around back where the mountain meets the house, the intersection of a temporary horizontal notion with a permanent vertical event. It's not an unpleasant place, a bit cramped, the trees are half dead. There's a small patio which is always it's shady and cool. I'd be glad to hang out back here if it wasn't for the fountain in the middle of the patio. I don't care for the fountain at all. A bronze naked mama sitting on a clamshell in a pool of water, one arm holding a baby, the other a pitcher from which water flows directly onto baby's face. The relentless gurgling is really quite annoying. The fountain is situated right outside the main dining room and at night it's all done up in dramatic lighting for diners who might enjoy an aqua-kinetic display of infanticide.

This is not the main fountain, however. The main fountain is on the circle at the top of the driveway. I don't understand that one either. Thematically, it's about horses, but just their heads, four of them, set around the edge of a round concrete basin at the four famous compass points. From the mouths of these disembodied equines the water does its gushing; mighty sprays aimed at a center column of clamshells where the water collects and cascades down to a pool of shimmering glass tiles. The whole thing is preposterous, mythologically and otherwise. According to Otto, the meaning behind the motif is if you don't like it, screw you. Besides being preposterous, the spray from the over-chlorinated water kills the flowers and most of the bushes planted around the circle. Fortunately for the flowers, the fountain is almost always broken, prone it is to the busted pump, the leaky pipe, the wobbly clamshell.

It's a bumpy ride, the back path, nothing but empty ruts of dry earth between the paving stones where grass is supposed to grow. Something they saw in a magazine. Otto is trying to explain to the Mexicans what he wants. It is a long and tedious exchange involving a number of languages, mostly made up. The Mexicans are highly resistant to the idea. They know what I know. Under the stones there's no dirt, only mountain. And there's no sunlight back here either. It's no place for grass, but weeds like it just fine.

At the end of the path before turning the corner toward the shack, I stop to examine what amounts to the stone house's rump, the southernmost end (by horsehead reckoning) of the edifice. For some reason unknown to me, and a topic that is rarely discussed (I believe a sore point rests here, unhealed and festering), this portion of the house was left incomplete, two floors unsheathed and roofless, save the lean-to like remnants of a beginning. Imperfect as my memory is (and a greater imperfection it is with each passing day), I recall toward the end of construction Otto nearly screaming his head off about it, at which point the machine with the long swinging arm went limp and the rock pounding ceased. The brown men and their bosses walked away and everything stopped. The increment was left undone and unrealized. They didn't even bother to clean up before they left. No fancy trimming, no walls of stone, a roofless two story wooden skeleton more like a mighty weed that came bursting up through the ground. The first floor serves as a shady place for the Mexicans to take their lunch break. The increment is the view from the porch of my shack.

My job is to put flowers in pots. A duty auxiliary to this is to put roses in vases. I work at a wooden table on the porch of the gardening shack, another shady place with a fan. Lilly tells me, *Be careful with those vases. They are very expensive. If you break one I'll take away your clippers and you'll have nothing to do all day.* She means it too. I don't mind the work. It is not borious. And I do the best I can with the vases.

The woman is very fond of roses. At the potting bench I arrange the cuttings according to size and color, then place them in the vases, same colors, mixed colors, whatever I like. Someone comes along to ferry the vases into the house. I can't say who...maybe the waitress, maybe the chef...not the Mexicans, not in the house. The woman places the roses in her all favorite places. *It fills the house with life!* she declares self-consciously, unsure of exactly what she should be filling the house with. If it's life she wants she should stick some weeds in those vases. Weeds are insatiably alive. The only thing weeds need to grow is neglect. Lilly hates weeds. Random nature intruding facilely on her perfect scheme. Roses, on the other hand, require more care than any other living thing on the mountain, including me. They are vain plants that embarrass easily. Even with the daily care they receive from the Mexicans, they will often chose to die just out of spite. Weeds must think roses the stupidest of plants.

Before I reach the door to the shack I come across Lilly arguing with one of the Mexicans—about weeds, no doubt. The Mexican leans forward, an attempt to better understand her instructions, she believes. Actually, he is trying to peek down her blouse. In the distance a car horn begins to blast, madly, hysterically. It sounds like it might be Otto at the gate. Lilly rushes to him. The Mexican does not. Perhaps he feels uninvited. I put my chair in gear and head toward the commotion at a pace not exceeding the manufacturer's recommendations.

FOUR

I PARK myself at the top of the drive by the horsehead fountain. The slope down to the gate is too steep for the chair, and I believe these legs have done all the walking they're going to do for one day. So I'll keep it right here. The horses are in standard malfunction mode this morning; the water is off and I can hear everything quite clearly from this safe perch. Below, I can see Otto and Lilly standing by the fancy iron gate which is closed despite Otto's car being close enough that it should have opened automatically, and even though the gate (like the fountain and most everything else around here) is broken all the time, it can be opened manually with the turn of a crank. But Otto hasn't done that. They both appear confused and highly agitated. From here I spot the source of their perturbation: wrapped around the iron bars where the two halves of the gate come together someone has secured a very serious looking bicycle lock.

Otto shakes the lock hard and yells goddamnit, while Lilly stands with her arms folded several steps clear of the calamity. Now Otto is on the phone, the police I believe or the army, and he is waving both his gesturing and phone hand which must make for a difficult conversation. It seems to be going nowhere. He dials anew and I hear the name Penzio, his sports car mechanic. *Make it quick,* he snaps and shoves the phone into his jacket pocket. For her part,

Lilly has made a tactical retreat to the car pretending its door required closing. She knows too well the magnitude of his simmering froth. One false move and he'll go up like a fertilizer factory.

But something altogether different and unexpected begins to emerge from this particular vent plume; through the steam and ash of first rage a flicker of calm overtakes the man (caught by my well-trained eye) and the furious stomping about has settled into a measured pacing between the gate posts. His hands, phoning and gesturing, are planted deeply in his jacket pockets. The head has taken a decidedly downward cast, eyes firmly affixed to the shine on his shoes. Lilly has noticed this odd change as well and has shortened the interval between them. Now each step takes on an importance all its own, tentative and terrifying in their deliberation, the calculation of heel to toe weighed with profound implications. What goes on in the man's mind no one can know for sure. We watch and wait. Beneath the wispy canopy of trees he paces back and forth as rays of pure white sunlight pour down upon his glossy skull. The blue of his suit and the red of his tie shimmer in the dappled gleam. He stops to assume a contemplative pose as though called to center stage by some great power.

He turns to Lilly and says, *Life is a series of adjustments, is it not?*

Yes, Ot, Lilly obligingly replies.

To myself I respond reflexively, *No.*

He continues, *The true measure of a man must be taken by how he reacts to the vicissitudes of fate, is this not so?*

Yes, Lilly tells him.

No, I say.

Are we not each of us the captain of a boat called glory? he asks, and out pops his gesturing hand. We do not reply. *Do we not beckon our glory and reject its gainsay? Or must we countenance each insult to it like fearful heathens and turn the other cheek? No, never, for this I will not do.* The man falls silent for the moment, the hand returning to the pocket. Then, in a rueful tone, he adds, *You know, not everyone wishes us well.*

And Lilly says, *I know, Ot.*
I myself am not aware that anyone wishes us well.

After a while, a deep throated rumbling comes up the mountain road. Penzio, to the rescue.

Penzio is Otto's Italian Italian car mechanic. He comes on a not particularly regular basis to work on the Italian cars Otto collects but never drives. I have no idea what kind of house he lives in as the topic of his living arrangements never enters his conversation. Every other topic does. Penzio could be Vice President of Talking. For the man and the woman, talking is also the chief preoccupation. From the moment they rise in the morning to the last conscious breath they take on their pillows at night they talk. They talk at breakfast with eggs in their mouth. They talk while they walk, while they sit, while they're lying down. There is no position they can assume that talking is not possible. They talk to themselves while sitting on the toilet or taking a shower. They talk while watching teevee. They talk while talking on the phone. And they talk all the time while other people are talking without regard for who is talking and what they're talking about. Just so they can talk. And even so, Penzio talks more.

Otto usually gets furious when someone walks around the gate. It's not even a wall they have to walk around, just a couple of block posts on either side, and all a person has to do is skirt themselves around a few cactus plants and they're in. Nevertheless, he has a visceral reaction to security violations. You're supposed to ring. That's what the button is there for. That's why there's a camera, so we can see your enormous nose on the little teevee screen in the kitchen. But the teevee screen is useless because the camera never works and the gate is usually jammed up with dead branches that fall from the trees that were planted in solid rock. Now Penzio walks around the gate and Otto can't say a word.

Penzio examines the lock. *Who do this thing?* he asks.
Dunno, says Otto. *Just get it off.*
This lock is for the beseeclett, Penzio tells him.

What do you mean, beseeclett? barks Otto.

You know... Penzio performs in pantomime the riding of a bicycle.

Just get the goddamn thing off, says irritable Otto. He's all finished being contemplative.

The mechanic starts up the drive. When he gets closer I can see that he's holding back a laugh.

Hey, Gustavo! Whaddya know, eh? I go get some tools.

What I know is that if Otto sees him laughing he will have a major meltdown. Penzio disappears down the ramp to the underground garage and reappears moments later rolling a big bottle of something and carrying a bag of tools over his shoulder. As he passes he says to me, *Come, you wanna see this.*

I haven't a monad of strength in my legs to follow him down to the gate. I can see just fine from here.

Penzio attempts to explain to Otto the nature of the difficulty.

This metal I no can cut, he tells him, shaking the lock and his head synchronistically for emphasis. *This is very special metal. This metal they use in space on the rocket ships.*

This explanation doesn't register with Otto.

Otto: *Whaddya mean you can't cut it?*

Penzio: *Itsa space metal, I tell you.*

Otto: *Bullshit.*

Bullshit is another of Otto's favorite things to say...about truth, not about evil. Otto has no favorite word for evil.

Penzio: *No bullshit, seenyourhay. Itsa too tough.*

Otto: *Bolt cutters. You know bolt cutters?*

Penzio: *See, seenyourhay.*

From the tool bag the mechanic retrieves an enormous pair of scissors. He presses the handles together and the fat little blades clamp down upon the neck of the lock. Penzio squeezes mightily, grunting and groaning for all he's worth and working up a real sweat, but the space metal remains intact, and before long he stands down.

Otto: *For crying out loud.*

Penzio: *I tell you, mister, she's too tough, like a rocket ship.*

Otto: *What about...whaddya call it, a hacksaw.*
Penzio: *Okay, we try the saw.*

Again Penzio digs into his tool bag and removes a device with a long, thinnish blade. He begins to saw across the metal, back and forth, harder, faster, but again, no luck and he stops, winded and bent over. Otto grabs the tool out of his hand and gives it a go himself. Furious penguin flaps wings frantically without flight. He cuts his hand and Lilly is right there at his side. She uses his handkerchief to bandage the wound which does not appear to be too serious, but it is significant in that the injury comes to his telephone hand.

Okay, Do the gate, Otto tells him.

I spy a thin smile crossing Penzio's lips. He rolls the bottle up to the gate, dons a big metal helmet with a little window in front, turns a knob and lights the tip of the torch. With a long blue flame Penzio cuts the iron bars of the gate and removes the lock.

FIVE

WITH THE TWO halves of the gate now unrestrained, Otto drives off without further pronouncement. Lilly returns to the house. I follow Penzio down the ramp into the underground garage.

The mechanic is no longer suppressing that laugh. He roars and guffaws. Laughing and coughing he says to me, *How come you no laugh, eh? You no talk, you no laugh. Whatsa a matter for you?*

Penzio wipes his hands with a dirty rag and fiddles with a coffee pot.

Your papa, he no like being in the jail. No like the locks. Somebody lock him up good. Itsa a very funny. Then, in a studied turn, *Who do this thing, Gustavo? Who put the lock on the gate?*

Penzio knows not to wait for my answer.

Your papa, he's a very angry man. All he wants is to go up and down the mountain in his big Nazi car, like an old goat. A goat in a blue suit.

He pours some coffee and leans against the door of my birthday car which he has yet to acknowledge.

I know about these angry men with too much money, Gustavo. The world she is full of these men. When I work at furraree we deal with these angry rich men. They no like this, they no like that. They want only what they want. Now, very very rich men, they no get angry, not themselves. They have somebody gets angry for them, so I think maybe your papa he's not so rich. In my country a man has a garage full of fancy cars he's a big deal. In America he is only a regular deal. That's a joke, Gustavo. You no laugh?

No, I tell him.

Okay, is not so funny. I try. I tell you a secret, Gustavo. That lock, she's not so tough. I take my grinder and in one minute, poof, she's off. But I tell your papa the lock is too strong. Space metal, I tell him...Ha! Can you believe, space metal! Thatsa a good joke, eh? Just to get the old goat mad. Whatta you think, I'm crazy, eh?

Yes, I say. And I agree, mad Otto is amusing. Penzio relocates himself to the front of my car and puts his foot on the bumper.

You crazy, I'm crazy, Your mama and papa, everybody they are too crazy in this world. And I tell you for true, your papa's garage is too crazy. What he is thinking? A palace under the ground with the marble on the floor and the candelabree and the fancy furniture. I am here and I think I must be in Roma or Venezea with the doge. How come and for what? Is too crazy in America when people everywhere live in boxes. This I no understand. And this window, Gustavo! (Penzio is regularly annoyed by this particular redundancy). *This big stupeedo window in the side of the mountain, to look at what, the view? Which is very nice, understand. It is most nice. But they have their view, right up there on top, on the peeatza. Why they need two views? You tell me. Itsa too stupeedo. Too much sun, no good for furraree paint.*

The mechanic loves furraree. That's what he calls the cars. Also, he hates fancy. So do I. Fancy makes me skittish.

I wanna know who cleans the window, eh? They must be some kind of mountain climbers with the ropes hanging down. I look at this window and I think, who gave their life to clean this window, because ropes break, you know, everything breaks. I think for sure, the last thing someone do in this life is to clean the window. This is too sad.

Penzio starts to laugh again and cough some more, probably because he's always smoking cigarettes. Otto does not smoke cigarettes. He smokes big fat cigars that smell like bathroom and he never coughs.

How come you get this car, eh? You no drive cars. The mechanic takes a slow walk around my birthday present.

Stupeedo English. You no like this car, eh?

No, I tell him.

I no think so. You a smart guy.

He opens the hood and inspects the engine. This disgusts him.

The name of this car is a cat in the jungle. But I tell you, itsa no jungle cat. This is a dog that stops every five minutes to smell its ass. Whaddya you think?

I don't know. He's talking about things I know nothing about. Cats, dogs, cars, the English.

Penzio turns a bucket upside down and takes a seat. I'm in for it now.

I tell you this, Gustavo, the first time I leave Eatalia I go to Yugoslavia. A very poor place, Yugoslavia. You no believe how the people live there. Too much work, too little money... the way of the world, God in his mercy. I am poor too and miserable, I no tell you why, and I get some work in the factory where is made the most biggest piece of shit car in the world. The Russians they no want this car it is too shit. And you know what job they give me? Me! They give me turn the screw. Yes, this is a job! Every day I stand there like a plant in a pot and down the line comes the shit car for me to turn the screw. Turn, turn, turn. Next car, turn, turn, turn. All day, I turn the screw. So I tell them, I am master furraree mechanic. And they say turn the screw. I tell them let me make your shit car not so shit, and they say turn the screw. I go crazy. I tell them turn the screw up the ass, and I go back to Eatalia which is very bad for me then but not so bad as turn the screw. You see, at furraree we no do it this way. We are no plants on the line, no standing in a box to do just one thing all day. At furraree the mechanic is like the bee, buzz buzz from car to car, you do this and that, and if it is not right you fix, you fix if you stay all night. And when the car she is finished you look and say, I made this and you feel good inside, good like you no feel for something else. Because you make art. Not like a man painting but like a man work-

ing. *Turn the screw* is how you say the opposite. Maybe you no understand this, my friend.

Vice President of Talking. Penzio rises from his bucket and slowly walks towards the main section of the garage where the cars are on display. He appears to be under some sort of spell. I can't see him anymore, but I can hear him, speaking perhaps to me, perhaps to the cars.

This one I make, a red head, kay bella...this one I no make. My papa he makes, for the races. No equal. Pisses on the English. This one, mazeratee. Okay, but not furraree. This one, lamb or geenie. Not so good. Unhappy factory, a little miserable there...

Imperious clip clopping. The woman approaches. She has the gait of a petulant autocrat.

The ensemble has changed. Now it's the red uniform, one selected from an incalculable number of red dresses in her closet which, when adorned with glittery spangly banglies and some shiny shoes, reminds her of how bad she is.

She's going to meet someone. A man, most likely. She does that.

Penzio has heard her too. He abandons his auto reverie and rushes to her like a sail caught in a personal wind. I hear him say *seenyoura,* and I hear some fidgeting and whispering, then some argue whispering. They turn the corner to where I am sitting.

Pointing to my birthday car, in her snappy voice she tells the mechanic, *Mr. Deal wants this car ready as soon as possible. He has decided to sell it.*

The woman looks my way as if to say...See, I got rid of the present we don't like. Great is my power.

Penzio replies, *Oh yes, seenyoura, he sells the car but I no can fix because this car it is too big piece of shit...I mean poopoo, missus.*

Why can't you fix it? I don't understand.

Well, I tell you why, he says, leading her around to the far side of the poopoo. *First thing, you go too fast, the wheels they fall off.* He whispers in her ear and she glares at him. He continues, *Also, the doors, they fall off too.* There's an exchange of decidedly heated whispering and Lilly returns to my side of things. Penzio stands at the car's open hood.

One more thing, missus, most important for true. Here where is the gasoline goes in for to make the spark...itsa no good. Very bad, very dangerous, seenyoura. You tell mister no to touch this car. First I fix or poof, big fire. Okay?

Yes, I understand, Lilly says.

Yes, big fire, he says.

Poof, says Lilly.

SIX

Yellow flowers, red flowers and blue. Orange flowers in crisp plastic packets. Plantlets, budding in a green bed, little plant children, robust and otherwise. Tangles of root hairs poking through the bottoms, seeking a more spacious accommodation. The spoon is a fine device—let go now—care must taken not to separate the tender stalk from its weak grip on the soil. I set out a row of the orange kind for a blue pot. Very fine. The soil smells delicious, better than any meal. I rub the soil between my fingers and admire the complexity of its texture, a remnant of the anonymous, the unspecified and unheralded, a life long deceased but decent enough to leave behind its nutrients for these hopeful fledglings. Old life for new, nature's perfect program spread out on my potting table to provide for my morning's occupation. This one I'll make and others, and the Mexicans will come along and take them away to distribute around the patio and along the walkways according to the woman's scheme. Or so I am led to believe. After awhile, she will order the pots emptied and returned to me to refill. New flats of earnest young petals will be brought to my table and full bloomed roses will be cut from their vines. These are the details of my enterprise.

The man and the woman are gone now; the man to his work, whatever that might be, and the woman to wherever and whatever occupies her day. I have no interest in their comings and goings. I don't wish to know at what enterprise they invest their lives. Every day they leave the house dressed in finery, intrepid, impatient to do a deed. They return only to eat, sleep, watch teevee and talk on the phone. They do not pot flowers or cut the grass or clean the house. Others do those things for them. Every so often there's a party. There are many things I do not understand, those events that exist beyond the driveway gates, all the urgencies, the demands of commerce. Money is a mystery to me. I lack the concept of quantity which is a failure of faculty or the absence of need. I do know that money is not as simple as having a dollar in your pocket. I am told often and pointedly that money paid for the doctors, many doctors. much money. They came from all over the world, the story goes. Viennese doctors, doctors from Tel Aviv. Specialists in the syndromatic arts and sciences. They came, looked me over and gave Lilly their diagnosis: Syndromes. I suspect there is more to it than that but that's all she can pronounce. Money wasted, according to Otto. Good money after bad, the oft-employed phrase. Otto makes sport of my reflexive disabilities. Sometimes he'll put a glass down in front of me just to watch me send it flying across the room—his personal rocket launcher. It sends him into spasms of laughter, but there's nothing I can do about it. Nor would I. I wouldn't mind losing the verbal tic, however. Making their yeses my yeses and their nos my nos is an involuntary accommodation, and it is unkind of him to make a toy out of me because of it. But then, Otto is not a kind man nor does he wish to be. At the breakfast table I listen to his phone conversations, only because it is nearly impossible not to, and through all the bullshits and goddamnits I witness how mad money makes him. He'll spit and hiss with a ferocious plume because the money is getting away, or is taken away, somehow it's not there or not enough is there; and it's always the others, all the others who are to blame for the denial of his claim to it. Such an angry, desperate enterprise it all seems to be. Money built his stone castle on the mountain, including that portion of it that money left unfinished. But he's never around to enjoy it. So what's the point? There are chairs he will never sit in, rooms he'll never visit, all those bathrooms he'll never know. The place is full of strangers all day long, cleaning and fixing things, moving this or that. Maybe they should live here. Use the pool. Someone should. Nor does he drive his fancy Italian cars sitting in the underground garage, his prizes, his trophies. Lilly says it's because he can't fit in them, but he fits well enough. When a new car is delivered to him, he'll first take a slow walk around it while it's still in the driveway, carefully examining the overall configuration of the thing. He will train his considerable powers of perception upon its angles and proportions, the quality of its demeanor, the negative space it displaces. His hands will explore its surfaces for signs of impurity or disease, the taint of imperfection, the infirmities of age, the ignominies of mileage or the insults of indifferent care. And he will kick the tires invariably because the mechanic says he doesn't know the first thing about cars, which I suspect to be true. Expertise his not his goal. His appreciation is limited to ownership which is all he requires. Before the car is taken down below to be put on display with the others, Otto climbs inside. An awkward moment to be sure, like the insistence that the shoe fits, but once inside there's no doubt he could pilot the thing if he wanted to. He'd rather touch the seats and rub the steering wheel, honk the horn and race the engine. He likes the sound these cars make. Their powerful rumble is in synchronicity with his own unique vibrations. They roar his proxy and he theirs. And even sitting mute and motionless on display, they perform as worthy agents of his exceptionalism.

Nothing is ever about what it's about. Everything is always about something else. Money doesn't work until it's turned into something other than money, transformed, transmogrified into a gleam, a glitter, a shine or a pile of something else before it's meaning can be fully taken. Otherwise, Otto wouldn't bother with the furrarees. Instead there would be piles of cash in the garage and visitors would be obliged to say *nice pile of dough you got there, kids*. People love piles of things, anything, dirt, stones, old tires. They are endlessly fascinated by them. The pyramids in Egypt are just piles of rock well organized. And once, long ago, money got turned into them. More bosses and brown men. And guess who didn't get to use the pool. That's what Penzio wants to know. He makes the same rant whenever I see him, rich angry men and turn the screw. I don't know what he really means by turn the screw. I do know that he's screwing Lilly, or was, but that's something different. I would explain to him that it happens that some jobs are by their nature repetitive, and it's easy to find yourself doing the same thing over and over again. At times, there's no getting around it. But it is the having to do it that rankles him. Obliging the money. Money doesn't like to be kept waiting. It doesn't wish to be interrupted. And don't ever make money mad or it will leave you roofless or wrap a bicycle lock around your gate. Space metal. I can't believe Otto fell for that.

The waitress and the French chef are crossing the lawn, heading straight for me. He's carrying a tray, she bears a bowl of soapy water and a towel.

Hey there, fella, the waitress says in a friendly, unexpected way. While her husband stands by holding my lunch tray all stiff-necked and put out, the new waitress gets right to the task of washing my hands and drying them with a fluffy purple towel.

Ain't supposed to be eatin' with your hands all dirty, but I've done it more than once and it ain' t so bad, she explains. The girl is remarkably energetic in her chores and in a flash I have in front of me not a pile of potting soil but a tuna fish sandwich and a cup of milk. The chef wastes no time in telling me, *Listen to me, missyour boy, you eat zee food, you no eat zee food, I am not caring. You knock zee food on zee ground, good for zee birds. I have no care. Do you wish to say yes?*

Yes, I tell him. The immobility of his neck is really very disturbing. My graceful arm is quiet.

The waitress chimes in, *Now Jock, there's no reason to talk to the little fella like that. He can' t help bein' a gimp and a retard and all.*

And all. She has no idea.

Also, language not being my thing, I can't be sure but I believe the waitress has acquired a different accent.

SEVEN

My pleasure in this life is a simple tuna fish sandwich. This is not it. The chef has completely frenched up my lunch and it is inedible. I swing my chair away from the potting table and retreat to the shack for a nap, which is also a pleasure.

The shack, the gardening shack, the guest's house, Gustav's little house--such are the names for my private place here on the side of the mountain. How I came to be installed here, who decided that I should live in these quarters and not in the house of stone with the man and the woman, I don't recall. The faculty of recollection is syndromatically in retreat, or more precisely, missing in action. Nevertheless, I am here and this is my abode. It is a simple structure, devoid of the fancy, the embellished, the lavishly adorned, more an unrealized increment to the grand scheme not unlike the butt end of the castle whose sticks and planks and rubble I view from my bedroom window. My roof is intact, however. The air conditioner works just fine. I have a lawnmower parked in the small living room, doubtless Otto's idea of therapy, the beginnings of my own personal stable of vehicles. I don't ride the thing and the Mexicans have their own push mowers to use, but here it is, more or less in the way. In what surely was meant to be the kitchen I have a sink and a small refrigerator which is regularly stocked with cheese and fruit and cold drinks so that I might be spared too many visits to the glasstop table. The bathroom is sufficiently wide to accommodate my chair although the numerous pulls and handles strategically located throughout makes the chair rarely necessary. The shower stall is exceedingly spacious and unenclosed to provide easy access. The bedroom contains the usual complement of furnishings: bed, table, lamp, dresser. I don't use the lamp much. I don't read. I can't. Perhaps I did once, epochs and eons ago. I can't recall. The bed is soft. The room is cool. I put my head down on the pillow and fall fast asleep. I dream...

...I hammer the clutch hard, give the handbrake a hard yank, and my mighty red scooteria does a saucy tarentella on the loose gravel of the parking lot. In the seat next to me Lilly is laughing her head off and waving her bebangled arms like a madwoman. Otto is waving an arm too, the gesturing one, although it is not clear where he's sitting because the car is only a two seater. I park where I want. The three of us march right up to the maitre d' who is most gratified and pleased to see us. Especially me. *How marvelous you can be with us tonight, monsieur. And your charming mother, bonsoir, madame. May I escort you to your usual table on the patio?*

As we pass through the restaurant everyone is eager to greet me. The men stand to shake my hand and the women wave calling out my name. Everyone is tremendously impressed with the gold braids on my uniform. We are seated at a round glasstop table open to the stars and not too close to the band. When the musicians spot us, they immediately strike up Lilly's theme song. She stands and takes a twirl for the crowd in her lovely chiffons which brings rousing applause. *Well done, Mother,* I tell her. Otto is on the phone now. His lips are moving but he doesn't speak. The atmosphere is very festive. The Mexican music fills the air, everyone is laughing and drinking, waiting anxiously for dinner to be served. The waitress appears at our table and asks me in a soft and gentle voice, *What'll it be?* The place turns stone silent. Not a soul stirs. Rising from the table I flash a wicked smile. All eyes are upon me now. I allow for a long pause, then, I proclaim it: Lamb chops for everyone! The patio erupts with cheers and clapping, hooray, hooray for Captain Gustav! In an instant, there are waitresses everywhere with enormous trays of bloody lamp chops. They load the plates of the ravenous patrons who begin scarffing the meat as if it were to be their last meal on this Earth. All talking has ceased and even the band has taken a lamb break. Only the sounds of chomping and slurping and gnawing can be heard. Otto is still on the phone, his mouth stuffed with meat. Lamb drippings are pouring down the front of his blue suit, covering his red tie. Lilly is also cramming herself full of lamb. Her lovely chiffons are soaked in grease. Like the others, she has dispensed with fork and knife and is tearing into the meat with her hands. She couldn't be happier. There is no food in front of me. My place is clear. I watch the reflection of the paper lanterns strung between the tables shimmer and dance on the patio stones now slick with juice and strewn with lamb bones. Nearby a portly woman holds a baby in her lap while stuffing herself with meat. The excess falls from her mouth into the child's and soon the baby begins to choke. No one seems to notice. All are too busy eating their lamp chops. Finally a waitress comes over and offers the woman a moist toilette, but now she is choking too. The band comes back from their lamb break and strikes up a happy tune. *Ole*, the people cry, *More chops!* The maitre d' leads a flock of lambs across the patio and all the people rise and follow the lambs into the kitchen. Soon the patio is empty. It's just me and Otto. He's been shackled to his chair by several heavy bicycle chains, his mouth full of meat and the phone resting on his shoulder. He begins to choke. Just before he expires he mutters, *goddamn heathens*.

EIGHT

THAT FIGURES. I dreamed one of Lilly's dreams.

As I lie in bed gazing out the window at two birds vying for a good spot on a nearby branch, I hear yet another commotion. More bicycle locks, I wonder? I get up to take a look. There are cops everywhere. Otto is home again, earlier than usual, and he has summoned the law.

From my bedroom window I can see Otto standing in the yard surrounded by a squad of very serious looking black-shirted policemen. They are combing the property, in and out of the stone house at every door, poking in the bushes, climbing the trees. I go back to bed, but no sooner can I put my head down on the pillow than I hear my door opening, with a bang. The cops are inside the shack. I listen to them buzz around the place like frantic insects looking for whatever it is they're looking for, but of course there's nothing to see here, including me. They come into the bedroom and lift up the mattress. *Nothing here,* proclaims one cop, probably the head cop, and the others file out (I can hear them at my work bench sifting through the potting soil). The head cop remains behind. I transfer myself to my chair. He stands directly in front of me, his hands on his hips, an arsenal around his waist. He says,

You must be the son, is it Gustav Arturo?

Yes, I tell him.

Am I sayin' that right?

Yes, I say.

Well, that's fine. He has the kind of voice that probably excels at yelling, mid-ranged, highly twanged. He is vaguely Neanderthal, thick forehead, broad nose, weakish chin.

Do you know who I am?

Yes, I say, although I don't.

Of course you do, You've seen me on teevee, I'll bet. Everybody knows their sheriff. Now Gustav Arturo, I'm gunna ask you some questions and I want you to respond, respond truthfully and to the best of your recollection. Do you understand?

Yes.

Good. That's very good. First, I want you tell me did you see who put the bicycle lock on the big iron gate?

Yes.

And who did you see?

I don't answer.

Who did you see put the lock on the gate, Gustav Arturo?

No answer.

The cop's voice raises a semitone and his uniform turns a shade blacker.

If you know something about this incident, Gustav Arturo, your are required by law to tell me, do you understand?

Yes, I say.

Then tell me, who did you see?

Of course, I don't answer. The cop is giving me a thorough stare down to which I am impervious thanks to the expert training I received from Lilly and Otto.

Do you understand there are severe consequences for refusin' to cooperate with an official police investigation?

Yes, I tell him.

And do you know that you could go to jail for interferin' with the law?

Yes, I say.

Then let me ask you one more time, who did you see put the lock on the gate?

The cop waits motionless for an answer that won't be coming.

Let me assure you, Gustav Arturo, jail would be a very bad place for a little muffin such as yourself, don't you think?

No, I say.

So that's how it's going to be. You fancy guys are all alike, ain't you? Think you're so graceful with your long hair and your beards. Well, you won't be gettin' any sympathy from me just cause you're in a wheelchair.

The cop is getting a bit steamed but he catches himself. His head drops down into his shoulders and he puffs a pointless sigh. Now he comes at me with a kinder, perhaps gentler tone believing he can catch me off guard, but he won't because I am not on guard.

Whatta we have here? A crime has been committed, an illegal act. Against this, your parents' house...your house. Someone did this thing. Who, I wonder? Who did this thing? Because it is my job as a sworn officer of the law to ponder about such things. Do your respect the law, Gustav Arturo?

Yes, I tell him.

The cop seems pleased with my answer. He smiles broadly with a mouthful of crooked teeth.

Why yes, of course you respect the law. We all respect the law. The law is what makes us free, don't you agree?

No, I report reflexively.

I think you are a very confused young man, Gustav Arturo. And maybe not so young as your mama would have us believe. Let me see if I can't straighten things out for you just a little bit.

The cop begins to pace circles around my chair.

You see, the law, which is to say, the rule of law, is the foundation of our freedom, Gustav Arturo. Without all the different kinds of rules and laws and statutes, prohibitions and injunctions we'd be no better off than the savages in the jungle. Just imagine yourself in that jungle for a moment, Gustav Arturo; it's hot and sticky in that jungle, a very unpleasant place and all sorts of bugs and nasty things are trying to take a bite out of you...

From behind the cop gouges me with a sharp finger to the arm. Ouch.

...cause you're such a tasty little morsel. Savages are everywhere. Savages and heathens in the bushes just waiting to jump out and murder you, steal your food, steal your personal property. Your personal property, Gustav Arturo! Do you extract my meaning here?

Yes, I say. I hope he doesn't stick me again.

I'm not sure you do. Personal property is another foundation upon which this great land of ours rests. The law and personal property. I can't say it strong enough. Why, without foundations like the one under that magnificent house out there, the edifice would come tumblin' down, now wouldn't it?

No, I am reluctant to tell him.

Hmm, he says. The cop grabs the back of my chair and begins to rock me slowly back and forth.

*The law exists, Gustav Arturo, the law exists to prevent our capitulation to savagery and heathenocity. It is there to prevent our recapitulation. First you've got your law...*he lifts the back of my chair...*then you got your order...*and lets it go with the thunk...*Now say it with me...*he lifts me again, higher...*your law....say it...*higher still...*and your order...I said say it...*and he slams me down hard. Now he tips me back toward him...*you're not sayin' it, Gustav Arturo...*he tips me all the way back until I am looking at him upside down. *You see this badge, fella?*

Yes, I tell him, though I don't. He's got a belly.

*What does it say? You're so smart. Tell me what it says on this badge? Go on, talk!...*he jerks me up and tips me forward so that I am certain I will topple out of the chair, but I hang on, then he slams me back down, spins me around and sticks his pockmarked face in mine. *It says security. Security of the personal property. Peace and Security. Your security. My security. Security of the homeland. Security and justice for all. It's the point I am trying to make to you here today. But I feel I am not getting through to you, am I?*

Yes, breathlessly I report.

*Well then...*and wheeling me into the doorway he begins to swing me from side to side, slamming me into the door jambs...*I'll* *ask you again*...bam!...*who put the bicycle lock*...bam!....*on the big*...bam!..*iron gate*...bam, bam!

Now he pushes me out into the living room and runs me in circles until I'm spinning like a top...*Tell me what I want to know, goddamnit. Talk, you little freak. Talk! Or I'll spin that beard right off your face*....

I have no reply for the sheriff and in short order he brings us to a stop. He's worn himself out spinning me around. His fat face is all puffy and red, and his eyes are bulging out of his head. He really should take a seat himself. Then an odd expression comes over him, and I'm not at all sure what he's going to do next. Huffing and puffing, he sticks his face in mine once again, and in a voice that is surely meant to be dark and menacing, he says to me, *Your mother will be very disappointed.*

I am actually glad to see Otto walk in the door. He retreats with the cop to a far corner and they speak in clearly audible whispers. The cop believes I am hiding something and Otto tells him about the war. I don't understand why he persists with this particular story. Is he so ashamed of the way I am? The cop backs down. Otto manages to lead him to the door. On his way out Otto tells me to stay.

NINE

Lilly has returned from her adventures in the red uniform. Because it is still my birthday, and because she is too tired to have the French chef cook for her, she decides they will go out for dinner. The man simulates an invitation to me and I decline by swiveling my chair and turning my back.

Instead, I have a bowl of spaghetti by myself at the enormous glass top table on the patio and view the view.

I am pleased to be alone. I am very tired with all that has happened today. I don't know anything about law and order. I prefer peace and quiet. It's hard to come by around here. I take a deep breath and endeavor to restore some order of my own.

There's a big moon out tonight. A birthday moon. All the lights are on in Paradise. A cosmos of flickering, glittering lights signals the general state of satisfaction. Patios are busy places after dark, when the desert cools and the umbrellas are lowered. Outdoor moments captured between the blazing sun and bedtime. Cocktails and talking, talking. Gratefully, I hear nothing. Only some dogs barking, far away. Perhaps they too are signaling. I notice several of my flowerpots have been placed at the edge of the precipice on the low wall that keeps the view viewers from falling over the side. The flowers are all wilted. No one has watered them today.

My quietude is broken by a blast of music coming from the house. The French chef and the waitress have the place to themselves and it looks like they're having a party, just the two of them. She's dancing by herself, still in her white uniform, her little apron and tiny white crown, and he's at the pool table lining up a shot. The music is very loud. The waitress appears lost in the song, and through the banging drums and strumming guitars I can make out only some of the words, a woeful tune about desperados waiting for a train. The French chef does not seem particularly moved by the desperados. He goes to Otto's bar and pours himself a drink. I watch to see if his neck moves. Oddly, it does not.

The spaghetti is tolerable, though it seems the chef couldn't help himself and has embellished it with a variety of unfamiliar and stinky cheeses. I am concerned this may become a problem.

The two of them are like hyperactive goldfish behind the glass of the game room doors. He looks very intense pacing around the pool table. The waitress comes flitting in, dancing with a bottle of beer and disturbs his concentration. He pushes her out of the way and proceeds to pocket the shot. I don't know how they can stand the music so loud. Banging and desperados, over and over. I've had enough spaghetti.

I turn my chair in the direction of the shack. As I pass the game room the waitress slides open the door. She's a little drunk, I think. She says to me, *Dontcha worry there, little man, cause there ain't nothin' to be worried about. You know why?* Before I could answer yes she puts her finger to my lips. *No, no. I'll tell you why. Ain't nothin' to be worried about at all because Jesus loves you. He loves you very much.* And she gives me a quick kiss on the lips and returns to her party.

I am having trouble falling asleep. Understandable, I suppose. Much commotion today. Many things were said, strange, inscrutable things, already slipping from my efforts of recollection. There was a lock, some kind of lock on the big iron gate, and later the cop came and told me I had disappointed my mother. The woman argued with the Mexican about weeds perhaps, or money. I don't know. I made some orange flowers in a blue pot which were most beautiful and I had a dream about driving a car and Otto choking on the phone. Did I see Penzio today? Maybe that was yesterday, turning the screw.

    I manage to sleep for awhile and when I awake it is still dark. I put my pants on and walk to the house though my legs are very weak. No more signs of a party. The French chef and the waitress have left. The house is dark except for the flickering of a teevee. I step through the kitchen into the teevee room. Otto and Lilly are on the sofa with their feet up on the table. I can't tell if they're sleeping, all crumpled up, still in their dinner clothes. They don't acknowledge me so they must be asleep although their eyes don't appear to be completely closed either. I can see in them the glint of teevee light. The show they may or may not be watching is about some people pretending to love one another. There is some kissing and some fighting. A man drives a red car and the woman wears a fancy dress. Otto and Lilly lie motionless, busy absorbing new lessons and new rules, new modes of behavior. They take it in like the dead absorb time. The teevee is their teacher and an instrument of temporary life support, but not for me. I watch this frantic light, pulsating, beating, staccato blasts of searing white light and I need to look away....flashing splashing rapid bursts of bright light and the ceiling begins to quiver...must look away. A man on the teevee says, *lately I've been getting frequent heartburn, and my doctor says it might not be heartburn at all but a symptom of a more serious condition*...the floor begins to quake, the walls swell, the room is being ripped apart. I lose my balance as I try with all my might to look away, but the lights beat ever faster, my muscles freeze and I drop to the floor, but I hardly have a sense of the floor...a searing pain, the light in my head like knives. I shake and gasp for a breath of air but I am lost...the tremor is upon me.

    What does it mean, the ticking of the clock? Time is meaningless, after all, the one thing that is about everything and absolutely nothing. The man and the woman have gone to bed. The machine is off and the room is dark. They've done all they can for one day.

What does it mean? The hour passed, the hour pending. Minutes are eons, and epochs but a flicker. If I relive the entirety of my life in a moment how do I know that my life did not take only a moment to live? And if I can't recall the history of me, how can I be sure that I was here or never here, that I didn't just appear one night out of nowhere, quivering on the floor in front of the teevee? What then is implied by the pages of a calendar? The fitful procession of numbers whose significance is lost to me beyond the tally of fingers, syndromatically canceled, struck dumb by affliction, rendered pointless by injury. How arbitrary the week, how absurd the month. The year calculated by an unworn shirt and the singing of the song. Happy, happy, endlessly happy. Meaning pressed upon meaninglessness. But time is indifferent to its calculation. It takes no notice of the laborious plotting of clock and calendar, and cares nothing for the duration of a thing so fragile as a lifetime. My time is near, or so I'm told. How shall I mark its passing? How will I know it's upon me?

A light from the kitchen stove guides me to the door and out of the house. My legs are beyond weak. They barely carry me home, and when I reach my bed I drop, exhausted. I fall deeply, dreamlessly asleep.

TEN

When I awake the sun is already well overhead and bearing down upon us for all it's worth. Twisting out of bed, I can't say for sure why my muscles are so sore. There's no telling what transpired in the distant past. Donning an old ball cap, I take to the chair and wheel myself around the property looking for sentient beings. No sign of Otto and Lilly. Only the sounds of birds in the trees, hiding out. The yard is devoid of Mexicans. The east patio is abandoned save two coffee cups that have not been cleared away. The kitchen too is empty, and I am aware that my stomach is growling. From the refrigerator I take a couple of slices of cheese and a cold plum. Very fine.

Through the house, I pass the dining room but not before taking a quick lap around the table; silken monks knelt in prayer before an enormous tree trunk, ignominiously felled. Just outside, mama's not drowning her baby today. She's broken again.

I reach maximum speed down the long marble corridor and do not bother with the paintings on the wall, for I have seen them before. Urns of fruit. A maiden tending a lamb. A man and a woman sitting on a rock under a tree. A cowboy on his horse. An Indian shedding a tear. All too silly to contemplate.

When I reach the front doors, the twin portals of glory, I turn to face what other see when first their muddy boots cross this grand threshold; splendor and unrestrained splendiferousness, the exaltation of fancy, fancy's international headquarters. Crystal chandeliers and marble stairways, a pair of them with a golden elevator in between for that third up/down option. Squiggles and fancy scrolls across the ceiling and down the walls. Stone columns the color of spinach and blood. Polished, sparkly, beaming, triumphant, the house, like its occupants, harbors no unvocalized thought. Nothing about it has gone unexpressed. It is entirely intended. A lumbering ogre, a gaudy virago. They have succeeded in making the world in their own image. It's what they do best.

I take the elevator to the upper floor and pass the library, its massive door perpetually closed, its hidden contents like wallpaper. The hallway extends in two directions; south to an incalculable number of vacant, forgotten bedrooms, and north to the masters' quarters. I turn north and soon hear the hum and blab of a teevee.

The monks' gift to posterity has been stripped of its sheets and its pillows piled high to one side. The babbling teevee is Lilly's and I roll around the corner to find the waitress on her knees scrubbing Lilly's toilet. She looks like a crumpled piece of paper there on the floor, her long white hair neatly tucked beneath her lacy little crown, the hem of her uniform pooled about her thin pale legs. She seems lost in thought scrubbing and brushing the bowl. Or maybe she's listening to the teevee. A man is screaming about being holy. His accent is a bit like the girl's when she's not being from Argentina. When the man yells, *Praise him,* the girl softly repeats to herself, *Praise him,* and turns to me as if she knew I was here all along.

I knew you would come, seenyour Gustav.

I am inclined to leave but when I touch the go button, the girl reaches out to me with a yellow gloved hand. *Please do not go,* she says. *I am hoping we can talk.* This sweet and gentle sounding other voice of hers is enough to oblige me stay for a moment and I turn my chair slightly in her direction. Sitting there on her ankles, her arm resting on the toilet seat, her hands encased in thick rubber and the sun pouring in through the garden window illuminating her small face, reflecting in her large brown eyes, I might think she was pretty. Prettier, certainly, than that other girl she seems to be when she's dancing or whatever that is all about. Our eyes meet and she smiles. Her thin, rouged lips are rimmed with a faint sadness, an expression I am not unfamiliar with on women.

There is too much in this house for me, she says, *Your mother must get another woman to help. I cannot do this all by myself.*

And the man on the teevee says,

"...*I feel his presence through the power of the holy spirit, right here, right now...*"

The girl closes her eyes and whisper mutters something to herself.

In Argentina my children are there. I must work for them to send money, may the lord preserve me. But I must not complain. We must not complain, yes, seenyour?

Yes, I tell her.

Your mother has told me about you, what she calls your syndromes. This is a funny word, syndromes. Your were not born with this, no?

No, I say.

When I hear this I begin to pray for you. I am praying for you this morning while I work. I am asking Hey Zeus Christo to forgive me for my selfish thoughts and to help seenyour Gustav that he might speak and walk again.

The teevee man says,

"...*a man who worked for his bread cutting stone came to the tabernacle to ask Jesus that he might heal him of his affliction...*"

The waitress lowers her gaze and does some more whispering. My eyes are drawn to her pale knees which the sunlight has turned the color of marble.

"...*and on the Sabbath day the lord said to the man, Stand forth...*"

I watch you planting your flowers. You make very pretty arrangements. The gardeners put them outside the windows so I can see them, They make me feel very happy. I want to know, please, are your happy, seenyour?

Yes, I say.

Do you understand me when I talk to you?
Yes.
Some people would say that to ask a stranger if he is happy is too personal a question.

"...show me your hand that I might heal thee, said the lord. And the man showed Jesus his withered hand and Jesus healed the man..."

When people say hello, how do you do, what must they mean if not, are you well, are you happy? I often think people do not say what they mean, yes seenyour?

Yes, I answer. More to the point, she has shifted her legs in such a way that the hem of her dress has begun a revealing retreat. I am not indifferent to such things.

"...Jesus Christ heals all who come to his tabernacle to seek his forgiveness, for he is the almighty, alrighty..."

Praise him, she mutters to herself. *You do not seem unhappy to me, seenyour, if I may say. But there is a sadness to you. I wonder if this is not a loneliness.*

"...I feel this Jesus right here on this stage standing right beside me, to guide me, through the night with a light from above..."

You do not have to be lonely, seenyour. The lord loves you. Hey Zeus Christo lives with you in your heart night and day.

Yes, I remember now. She said Jesus loves me, when she was dancing, when she was being somebody else. Now it's the lord and God and Zeus Christo who love me too. About all this I know absolutely nothing.

"...holy, holy, holy, lordy the lord is holy; the whole world is chocked full of his glory..."

Sometimes I feel lonely. Can I tell you this?
Yes, I tell her.
I have no friends here in America. Only Zhock, my husband. But a husband is not always a friend. Marriage must be this way sometimes. There are things I would like to tell someone, someone kind who will listen and understand. My heart aches to speak these things. Does your heart ever ache to speak what is in it?

Yes, I am obliged to say, but I don't believe it does.

"...*I waited patiently for the lord and he inclined to me, and heard my cry...*"

Her hand falls from my hand and rests on my knee. *Ask the lord to forgive you, seenyour. You must pray for forgiveness and open your heart to him, open it fully, open it wide.*

"...*my grace is sufficient for you, for my power is made in weakness...*"

You must ask God, seenyour, and he will hear your words. Unlock your heart and let Hey Zeus Christo in. His love will fill your soul. God's grace will heal your afflictions.

"...*So it will be at the end of the age; the angels will come forth and take out the wicked from among the righteous...*"

The waitress is getting a tad flushed with all this talk about her three friends. I understand she is talking about her deity, about God. This much I know. But really, how many of them are there? I also know that in the process of describing how I might get myself involved in the program she had managed to loosen the top button of her uniform and a bead of perspiration is working its way down her neck into the darkened cleft. She is on her knees now, her yellow gloves are on my lap and her slight but altogether normal nose is uncomfortably close to mine.

Then pray with me, seenyour Gustav. Pray with me to the lord God Hey Zeus Christo...

Oh, I see now. They're all the same. It's a name thing. No faster way to confuse the issue than to give a thing a name. I have several myself. Call me Gus and I'm a racecar driver. Call me Gustav and I'm a Viennese psychiatrist. Otto calls me captain. That's three right there.

"...*and he shall be known by the name which has no name....*"

Say this prayer with me, you poor, poor man. Say it.. Dear lord, I feel your love flow through my body like a river. I shall be yours until time has no meaning. Hey Zeus, hear us and heal this man. Heal him of his terrible syndromes. Restore his legs that he may walk beside thee...

"...*and no good thing will he refuse them who walk upright...*"

Restore his speech that he might sing thy praise...

"*...and the afflicted people thou will save, but thine eyes are upon the haughty, that thou mayest bring them down...*"

She's placed her whole head in my lap while she talks to her lord, and I can smell her hair, flowers and ammonia.

Holy father, heal this wretched man, this most gentle lamb of your loving flock...

Well, that's it. It's always about lamb soon or later. I rise up from my chair and step away. The girl falls backwards, astonished for some reason. As I'm leaving I notice there, in the dressing room, a pair of shoes full of Lilly's toes. The woman's game. I flee in haste, faster than these tired, unreliable legs should ever have to take me, having found the topic of the girl's oratory, to wit, Gustav's syndromatic self, roundly unpleasant. All those lords. In the future she should endeavor to keep both her faces out of my lap.

ELEVEN

THE ESTATE IS IN A STATE. Where are the roses, clipped and delivered to my table? Where are the flats of budding flowers for me to put in pots? The Mexicans are supposed to bring them to me. They are supposed to do a lot of things around here, like cut the grass and blow the leaves, clip the bushes and remove the weeds. But when I look about I see that none of these things has been done. The place cut use a haircut and a shave. I can't imagine how Lilly has allowed this to happen.

The Mexicans have gathered at the unrealized increment, more of them than usual by my imperfect reckoning, and they don't appear to be interested in taking up their work. Instead, they have brought their families here and are setting up camp on the second floor. I hear the giggling of children at play. I can't remember if there's ever been a child on the mountain before. We're about grownups here.

Fat puffs of smoke begin to rise above the structure and I catch the pungent, acrid smell of searing flesh cooking over an open fire. A loud radio plays a jolly tune. The clatter of men laughing and women yelling at children and the kids yelling at one another has overtaken the quietude.

Enter Lilly, striding purposefully up the walkway, an angry sort of clip clop. She heads straight for the increment and locates and engages the head Mexican, a stocky fellow in a tee shirt and ball cap. It's impossible to make out what she's saying but I can see she is having some trouble. Unable to communicate in a common language, the two resort to hand gestures, which are surprisingly translatable. Lilly makes a wide arc with her arm in opposing directions and brings both hands together in a pointing motion (What do you people think you're doing here?) The Mexican opens his arms wide and throws his head back (Hey, lady, what's your problem?) Lilly scrubs the air in front of her (You can't stay here.) The Mexican pats his pockets, shrugs his shoulders and shakes his head (You no pay, we no go.) Lilly shakes her head right back at him and points to an unspecified location in the distance (Get out of here right now.) The Mexican points to himself, to the collection of other Mexicans in the ruins, then to the ground immediately in front of him (No, lady. We stay right here.) Lilly takes her phone out of her pocket and stabs at it several times with her finger (Go on, or I'll call the cops) The Mexican tosses his hands in the air and makes a face (Call the cops. See if I care.) Lilly shakes her sharp finger in the man's face (I'm telling you for the last time.) The Mexican returns the finger shaking and makes a curious gesture with thumb and forefinger (perhaps another version of no pay, no go.) Lilly scowls mightily, throws her hands up and walks away (Jesus Effing Christ) The Mexican turns to his clan who have been watching intently from behind the ruin's wooden carcass and raises a fist in the air which is received with a hearty cheer (We stay!)

It would seem I have some new neighbors.

TWELVE

THERE's a man by the pool. A man of some sort, a little fellow, standing by the pool, looking lost. From my porch it's impossible to tell who he is or what he might be up to. Another in a series of deliveries perhaps. The incremental satisfaction of the woman's every desire. He looks like the delivering type in his ball cap and sneakers. What's he doing by the pool? Came around the gate no doubt when no one answered the bell. Now he's lost in the chaotic bombast that is our unhumble abode.

I suppose I shouldn't be concerned. Not a moment goes by that one or another stranger isn't roaming around the place, fixing this or that or cleaning up one of the masters' messes, poking his nose into some preposterous dilemma. This is because great big houses have great big problems. Attention must be paid. Care must be taken. The castle sits up here on the mountain like a transplanted organ in constant peril of rejection. Recently I have sensed that the parade of these service phantoms has dwindled to a crawl. Messes are piling up and what breaks stays broken. No one is ringing the bell to announce they have to come to rectify the latest discombobulation. Soon the mountain will decide it has held up the house of stone long enough, *I have held up this stupid thing long enough,* the mountain will say, *Now away with it!* And the mountain will slap the house down with its bony palm, down the canyon and into the valley so that all the stones from Italy can begin their journey homeward.

I wheel myself off the porch and head toward the pool, but the little man has vanished. Very odd. I would have seen him if he moved back toward the house. Where did he go? For no other reason than the weary curiosity that sometimes solicits my attention with life on the mountain, I decide to press on. Around the pool, back behind the pool house, down the grassy slope to the lower garden. No sign of the wayward delivery man. I stop to inspect the site of Otto's personal landscape project, another periodical inspired disaster, what he calls the hedge maze. No dirt, no water, the plants were doomed at the idea's conception. Not a single shrub managed to grow taller than the armrest on my chair before shriveling beneath the horrific sun. All that remains of the man's dream of deep verdant tunnels is a yard full of kindling and a healthy crop of weeds. On the other side of this sorry spectacle I spot the little man running back towards the house, and I double back to catch him.

When I come around again to the patio, I find the man sitting at the enormous glasstop table, taking in the view. My instinct is to flee, but the man turns to me and speaks, *Come, young man. Sit by me. Let's visit for awhile.*

I am not inclined to visit with the delivery man, yet I find myself pulling up to the table's edge as if drawn there by a lateral expression of gravity.

The little man is even smaller than I had first reckoned and far older than any delivery boy I can recall seeing. His ball cap is absurdly large on his furry ears. He is well on his way to fossildom.

Maybe you know who I am, he says in a gravely old man voice. He poses the question in the form of a statement to which I am not obliged to reply. *Maybe you've seen me on teevee.*

So many teevee stars lately. The last place I would have seen him. We sit while he views the view.

Then, through his tight, grimy smile he says to me, *Well, I suppose I should introduce myself.* Concentrating on the particular nastiness of his crusty lips, I miss some of his name, but I catch the last part, Vice President of the United States, and immediately I think he has come for his lamb chop chef. *And you must be the son, Gustav.*

I am obliged to say nothing.

Your mother has told me a little about you (I should have known). *That's a fine name, Gustav. A strong name. After your grandfather, I'm told, also a soldier* (Not that. Otto's the one who tells that tale.) *No matter that he fought for the other side. Honor is honor, and it's honorable to be a soldier, to serve and fight for one's country, whichever country, and we honor those who fought and fell or stumbled, gallant warriors regardless of stripe who deserve our thanks for beating back the heathens, the enemies of freedom, our freedom or theirs. Am I right?*

Yes, I am obliged to say.

Yes. Of course. And Gustav is a good name for a brave soldier. Gallantry, honor, bravery. The heat of battle. Glorious victories against the heathens and naysayers...oh, to be young again. I envy you, invictus,/ Out of the night that covers me, /black as the pit from pole to pole, /I thank whatever gods may be for my unconquerable soul. Do you know this poem?

Yes, I tell him though I have no idea what he's talking about.

Of course you do. Your mother tells me you used to read quite a bit. Well, books are one thing, but bravery and honor are quite another.

.../It matters not how straight the gate, how charged with punishments the scroll./ I am the master of my fate, /I am the captain of my soul...

Sure, that's it. Liberty and justice. That's what it's all about. The heat of battle, not some books. Honor and glory, serve and stumble if need be. No matter how straight the gate. That's what I say, the bludgeoning of chance, you gallant warriors, regardless of stripe, you captains of the common fate, whatever gods may be. Am I right?

I clench my teeth and tell him, *Yes.*

Yes, yes, that's the spirit! I knew we'd see eye to eye. Two soldiers, though I never served, a statesmen in my youth, we fought them off, the naysayers and the enemies of freedom, my pen, your sword, words and deeds, the last full measure of devotion right between the eyes, we took 'em down, didn't we, son? (a no, like a hiccup catches in my throat). *The heathens, oh, the heathens...God hates heathens, did you know that, boy?*

Yes.

Did you know that?

Yes.

God hates 'em for sure, but he loves glory. Oh, how he loves it. Why, that's why we got us some liberty, liberty and justice. Invictus, glory! Never mind the wrath and tears, pay no heed to the black pit, the horror of the shade...though my face be marred with dust and sweat and blood, brave soldiers were we, no matter what the stripe, no matter how straight the gate...a full measure of it, that's what we gave 'em. Sure, read the scrolls, read the books. Everybody's got a book. I got thousands but I don't read them. Heathens write books too, and there's no honor in that. No honor in being a naysayer. God hates naysayers. Am I right?

Yes.

Of course I'm right. Heat of the battle. That's what he loves. Be all that you can be, that's all he's asking. No wincers, no crybabies. No glory in that. Sure, the brave stumble. They stumble all the time. But they get right back up, right back in there, once more into the breach, that old arena, cause that's what it's there for. Honor and justice, the unconquerable soldier, the dusty faced warrior, whatever the stripe, whatever gods may be, one for all and all for the common fate, captains and masters, fighting for truth and justice, right there in that old arena, glory, glory hallelujah, that's what I'm talking about, the rocket's red glare, for which it stands, that's what God means, the truth keeps marching on, that's what he's trying to tell us. Nothing wrong with you boy that a haircut and shave won't cure. Just remember, these are dangerous times. I'm glad we had this talk.

The Vice President has concluded his remarks.

I put the chair in reverse and slowly back away from the table, concerned that he'll go off on me again. But his gaze is no longer on me. It is on the view. I make it off the patio and onto the walkway, and just as I am ready to slam it into high gear and make my escape I see Lilly there behind the game room doors. She's been watching all the while. I realize of course that like prayer time with the waitress, this encounter was her doing too. She's been very busy lately. My therapy coordinator. My character coach.

THIRTEEN

I PASS through the garage thinking maybe Penzio's around. I'm not sure why exactly. Perhaps I require the perspective of an overwrought Italian anarchist right about now to take my mind off the going over Lilly has put me through lately. But the mechanic is nowhere to be found. I check his usual napping places, the backroom, the storage closet, the car with the seat that folds down. No Penzio. It seems that in a very short space of time everything is changing.

The ramp up from the garage is plenty steep and I can feel the chair is running out of juice. I'll need a charge soon. I manage to make it to the top of the drive when I hear the clank of the dismembered gate opening and in drives Otto. Lilly has appeared on the scene too. When she sees me she rushes right over to say, *Daddy called and said he has a present for you,* in her best let's-get-excited-together voice. If I had the power I would blow on out of here right now. I wonder what kind of shape my legs are in. But it's too late to flee. Otto parks his big black car right in front of me and there's no escape. I'll stick around to find out what he's come up with. I never did get my pants.

Come 'er, boy. Got something for you. Otto opens the back door of the car. It is not a pair of pants. Lying on the seat is a very large, very hairy black dog. Lilly says, *Jesus Effing Christ*. Otto explains that the dog is in fact a highly trained, very expensive guard animal, and its addition to the overall security paradigm will far outweigh the extra effort required to allow boy the privilege of thinking he owns it. The boy will undoubtedly benefit from the companionship of the beast and who knows, maybe he'll learn some responsibility from the experience. Just maybe it'll knock him out of his syndromatic funk, whatever the hell that is. Otto is quick to qualify the possible advantages for the woman but he won't be boxed in by any promises. He's not looking for a fight. More to the point, he doesn't really care what having a dog might do for me. Otto has written me off, as one of his business phrases goes. What we learn in the testy exchange between the man and the woman is that the dog may not be so highly trained as it is unwanted, a cast off from one of Otto's employees with too small a house for such a massive animal.

Lilly's objections, expressed through a familiar series of pained facial gestures and caviling non-sequiturs, places the gift in the same category more or less with the birthday car. *It is inappropriate,* she states, which is a strange word for the polysyllabically challenged woman to use; it comes out of her mouth like an obscenity. She raises the issue of her allergies which are varied and plentiful. None of this has an effect on Otto who has already decided that the dog stays. The waitress will help boy look after it and chef will feed it. Discussion over.

The dog, for its part, will not exit the car, and by this I attribute to it a measure of the finest sort of judgment. Otto attempts to command the animal out, *C'mon dog, let's go. Out, out...get out of the goddamn car!*

Otto's bluster makes no impression on the dog. Its supine length is barely contained on the sofa-like car seat.

Does it have a name? Lilly asks.

She called it Jeffrey or James or something. Dunno, he tells her.

She did, huh? Is that what she called it? Maybe you should have her get the dog out.

Otto gives her a hot glare but does not respond.

Those are stupid names for a guard dog, Lilly continues. *Who's going to be afraid of a dog named Jeffrey?*

Call it whatever you want, the man tells her.

Let's call it Cindy, the woman suggests which initiates a long and heated exchange regarding the nature of Otto's acquaintance with the dog's former owner.

Now it's Lilly turn to call the dog. She inches up to the car, but not too close as she is clearly discomforted by the beast. She bends down slightly as though she were addressing a small child.

Hello there, Jeffrey or James, she offers, to which the dog lets out a mighty bark that puts Lilly back on her heals. Apparently it doesn't care much for those names. I know how it feels.

Lilly says to me, *Gussie, do you want to call the dog?*

When I answer *yes* the dog comes bounding out of the car and right up to me, gives my leg a quick sniff, then goes over and pees on the nearest rose bush.

FOURTEEN

I DON'T KNOW about you, dog, but I'm beat. I have to go lie down. You can follow me if you want, otherwise you're on your own. My actions serve as my words and I trust, like the others, you'll understand this.

I take the back way to the shack past the fountain family mother and child along the edge of the mountain. The dog seems only mildly curious about me and my sluggish chair, preferring instead to give all the nooks and crannies along the way a thorough smelling. When we turn the corner of the increment I am reminded that the Mexicans are here now. From the top floor I can see the bare legs of children dangling over the edge. They appear most interested in the arrival of this black beast. The dog gives the kids the once over and returns his significant nose to the ground. I give the scene a wide berth as the commotion is too great. I am ready for that nap I've been trying to take all day and I wonder, with all that has happened to it today, if the dog isn't ready for a nap as well. I open the shack door but I can't tell if the dog intends to follow me in or if it's at all interested in being inside. What I don't know about so many things, including and especially dogs, has suddenly become an immediate problem. I leave the door ajar but the dog declines my halfhearted invitation and instead folds itself into a comfortable flop on the porch. My power chair gives out before I reach the bedroom and I have just enough steam in my legs to get me to the mattress where I too so flop. I begin to dream…

…Resplendent is the cathedral, an edifice of pure light and glittering gold, of towering marble columns and glowing panels of stained glass. The music is glorious, from Bach's Magnificat, sung by a choir of invisible angels, *et exultavit spiritus meus in Deo salutari meo,* and everywhere vases of roses, glorious white roses, filling the chapel with life. But the church is empty, save the singular figure of a woman who stands at the alter, waiting. She wears a gown of silk and lace with shiny slippers and gold ribbons entwined in her flaxen hair. She feels quite special in her lovely costume, but she's clearly troubled by something and chews on her fingernails without regard for her expensive manicure. I've waited so long for this day, she thinks, so why do I feel so bad? I could use a drink. She wonders if they serve in these places, unfamiliar she is with this strain of worship. A drink and a smoke. No more of that after today. And a pill. One of those little blue ones that calms a person right down. He'll have no more of that. So let's get it over with already. Where the hell is he, anyway? And how did I get here? Everywhere you turn there's Jesus on the cross staring at me like everything is my fault. Does he even believe in this stuff? He never mentioned all this Jesus stuff before. Now suddenly it's all over the place, and the minute I say I do I've got to wonder, I do what? Not too much of this, I hope. We don't do this where I come from.

    There he is, finally. All the way in the back. Taking his sweet time loping up the aisle by himself. I don't think we're doing this right. I'll bet there's all sorts of weird shit coming my way. Look at him, will you? That tux, like something left over from the prom. I'm marrying the homecoming king, for crying out loud. Lucky me. Goddamn lucky me. What a schmuck. Well, hurry up, your majesty, and somebody turn off that stupid music. It's giving me a migraine. Yea, that's right. Stand next to me, you big dope. Where do you think you stand, down the street? And who's this other old fart standing under the big Jesus giving me the evil eye. Get a load of that get up, will you. Looks like he's wearing Bubbie Finklestein's bathrobe. What a putz. I got to get out of here. I'm sorry, but I can't marry you today.

But mein leiben Lilly silly filly...vas is da fuss? Eine fine you lookenzie und hotsy totsy fur der nachtbangen. En zie finger I puttenzie da ring. Sayenzie ya. I sayen ya. Wunderbar! Das is dat. We danze. But first, zie snouthooken es nicht, mein leiberlilly. Sittenzie acht ein der grossen chairen fur das straightenhaben der schnozzlejuden.

The woman cries out but her voice has no volume. She feels the air being squeezed out of her by the crush of the man's monstrous arms. Once more she attempts to call for help. From the depths of her soul a sound churns and gurgles, struggling for liberation, the tongue seeking synchronicity with the lips, her lungs pushing, urging her scant breath toward the fugitive vowel, the elusive consonant, desperate to summon her salvation. With tears streaming makeup down her cheeks, she is waltzed down the aisle by the man who is by any measure an unusually large homo sapiens and exceedingly clumsy. Her feet hardly touch the floor, and when he twirls her about in his ungraceful way, her ankles bang against the...what do you call them? Pews. She would have to learn about all that now. So much to learn.

The enormous double doors of the cathedral swing open and now the woman is standing alone in a new place, the grand ballroom of an enchanted palace. Crystal chandeliers, marble the color of rubies, and in the balcony an orchestra, playing her song. She's wearing that sexy little number in red that shows off her perfect curves. The music swells and touches her heart. And there, across the scarlet sea amid the shadows waiting, waiting for her...the one, her lover. She runs to him and he to her in a frenzy of desire. She falls into his tender embrace, dissolving in a fountain of tears and sighs as her lover strokes her claret curls and plants kisses on her head.

Why, she pleads, *tell me why it must be this way?*

And the man says, *because, ma bella testarossa, the mind, she is a heathen mad for her own demise.*

Not exactly what the woman wanted to hear. She steps back and brushes herself off.

I don't know about that, she says, *I mean, you're being a little melodramatic, don't you think?*

It is very infortuno, I agree, senora, says the man. *But it is what it is. I cannot help what is the truth.*

Well, then let me tell you something infortuno, bub. Your anarchy is nothing more than a subterfuge to mask a deep psychical wound which you attribute to class bigotry but which is nothing more than common envy and the frustration of unrealized personal development. You talk about the truth, the famous truth, as if it were utterable only through your lips, out of your heathen brain.

The man says, *Take off your clothes.*

Yea, yea, sure. And she begins to disrobe. *She is a heathen mad for her own demise...Give me a break. Who even talks like that? How long have you been in this country anyway? Have we seen your papers?*

You are forgetting one thing, my darling, says the man.

What's that?

You are not this smart.

Oh.

Now the woman is transported to a place in the garden that does not exist except that she saw it once in a magazine. A hedgerow maze, the type favored by European royalty on lavish estates. She is standing at the entrance to the maze, barefoot and wearing a sheer nightdress. A voice calls out to her. She turns and sees the housekeeper who is mostly naked herself except for a starched white apron and that flimsy little crown she has to wear on her head. Dark clouds are forming and a cool wind stirs....

Ya shouldn't be listenin' to the Eye-talian mumbo jumbo, ya know, says the girl. *That greaseball's just trying to scare ya so he can get in yer pants.*

What is this place? the woman asks.

Why, don't ya know? It's the labyrinth.

The...what?

For cryin' out loud. I swear, more than two syllables just confounds you, don't it? Labyrinth, labyrinth. Say it with me....

Latter-binth, Lilly says.

Ain't no such thing. Slowly, lab-yr-inth.

Laby-rinth, she repeats.

Good enough. See, ya ain't so stupid after all. But ya gotta learn to concentrate when ya talk. That's the key. Don't just spout out every little noise that comes into yer head. Makes ya sound like some kind of moron.

Lilly turns back to the entrance of the maze.

What am I supposed to do? she asks.

Well, my guess is yer supposed to go in it. That's what them things are fer. To go in 'em. Don't ya think?

I'll get lost.

What are ya talkin' about? Take a proper look at it. Them bushes don't come up to yer knees for christsakes. Poor things, they're half dead. Didn't nobody tell ya, ya can't plant stuff in rock?

But when Lilly looks into the mouth of the labyrinth she doesn't see the scrawny little shrubs the girl is talking about. Instead she is confronted with a dark tunnel of towering hedges, forbidding, inscrutable, threatening to swallow her into oblivion.

I'm afraid, she cries, although she has already taken her first steps into the maze. And the evermore distant voice of the girl comes back at her,

So what else is new?

FIFTEEN

I wake with a start, not from the dream so much because that was obviously another one of Lilly's and a particularly stupid one too, but because the dog is now in my bedroom, sitting by my mattress and giving me a genuine stare down.

Up on an elbow, I take my first good look at the beast. A real monster, for sure. On its two back legs I suspect it would be at least as tall as me. Tight ringlets of dense black fur cover its entire body from tip to tailless rump. Atop its massive head two stiff little triangles seem comically insufficient to serve as ears and its great jaw is framed by a thick beard (not unlike my own). Something like a mustache hangs down over the mighty maw like old peasant whiskers. Neither contour of joint nor delineation of paw can be discerned on this solid animal, and I conclude from its most prominent feature that what it does best is smell. The nose is quite grand. Through the thicket of hair on the brow I detect the merest suggestion of oculi. Perhaps we are making eye contact. There is no way to know for sure, but the dog breaks into what might be construed as a smile, a dog smile, as good as any, the protrusion of fat tongue and a steady huff-huff.

All this is well and good except that I need to make a trip to the bathroom, and I find that my legs are unable to bear my weight, a syndromatic inconvenience, the fickle coming and going of capacity. With no chair in sight, I am obliged to drag myself across the floor. Does the dog sense my difficulty when it rises with me and begins to turn in circles as I crawl towards the door? It seems highly amused. Taking advantage of my compromised posture, it lays a big wet lick across my face. When I push it away I am surprised how pleasantly soft it is and how gently it yields to my touch.

In the bathroom I avail myself of its many handles and pull bars to accomplish the task, but once completed I am down on the floor again squirming like some sort of decrepit reptile into the main room in hopes that someone has been decent enough to come around with my chair. All the while the dog nudges and prods me along, rendering its interpretation of assistance.

The door to the shack opens. It is the French chef with a delivery.

Missyour boy, you are all over zee floor. Zees is no good, no?

No, I am obliged to agree.

Ma damn mommy say I am bringing you zee chair.

The chef has brought one of the spares, a non-electric model.

Zees one is to push. Too bad for you. Maybe you need zee help.

Clearly not a question. The bastard knows I need zee help though he makes no move to provide me with any. Decent of the dog to sit by me while I lift myself up using its sturdy shoulders.

See, you no zee help. You have zee doggie. You like zee doggie, yes?

Yes, I say, which is more than I can say about him.

I tell you something about zees doggie. Zees dog is from la France which is my country in zee Europe, but you do not know about zees things, of course. Zey use zis doggie for to gather zee cows. Maybe doggie will gather missyour boy into zee kitchen for zee tuna fish sandwich which I make special way for you. Is ready now, you come.

As the French chef leaves I contemplate my first command as dog owner. Kill. The gesture I make goes unobeyed.

The dog's food, uniformly and nuggety, is placed in an ample silver bowl on the east patio just outside the kitchen door. By the looks of things the dog doesn't care for its dinner any more than I care for mine. The French chef has seriously overthought the concept of tuna. The thing is inedible. Naturally, Lilly is no where in sight. At least she understands how to prepare a simple tuna fish sandwich, and I'm sure she would admonish this kitchen cretin if she saw the fancy he put all over mine.

Missyour boy does not like zee tuna?

NO! There are times when a resounding no feels quite satisfying. I wrap the sandwich in my napkin, put it in my pocket and open the door for the dog. C'mon. Let's get out of here.

I decide to take another look for Penzio. The fridge in the garage occasionally yields a decent pear. But there's a problem; the dog will not get in the elevator. C'mon, I gesture. It's not as dangerous as it looks. But the dog stays put. So I decide to leave it and go myself. As the car begins to drop I watch the dog watching me. An odd sight for an animal, to be sure; a room suddenly being swallowed up by a house like it took a big bite out of itself that happened to include me. How could it ever trust the floor again? I don't feel right for leaving it behind.

The garage is almost completely dark. Strange, as Otto insists on keeping his toys under the spotlight. No good, he says, natural light from the big window all wan with easterly sentiments. No good, he says, the inconvenient irregularity of the sun. Otto prefers those stark white light bulbs that make sharp black shadows and cast each car as itself and its umbral twin. Minus the illumination, the cars seem sinister, like big-nosed jungle cats crouching in the bushes, ready to pounce.

Cautiously, I maneuver my manual ride through the formation of darkened furarrees and head toward the section of the garage where the mechanic does his work. Perhaps I hear a knock or a bump or a shuffle. There's a light on in the corner, a lamp at the workbench. Penzio? I sit very still for a moment listening. Nothing.

I'm thinking about the dog I left upstairs and how it wasn't very fair of me to go off like that with Lilly lurking about. Not much of a guard dog, won't take a simple elevator ride. I could use it right about now to sniff around this dark cavern for an Italian. The stairs are out for me, my legs don't have an ounce of juice in them. There's the ramp down from the driveway. Usually a might too steep. The electric could handle it, but I don't know about pushme here. It's taking a long time to charge. I'll go back for the dog.

When the elevator opens onto the main floor I hear in my immediate proximity a hellacious scream, the woman's personal pitch. Skidding quickly into the living room I see Lilly and the dog—the dog being the principle problem. Its significant furry self is stretched lengthwise across one of her incomparably special sofas which she must always refer to by both name and price. Lilly is using all manner of her limited vocabulary at the loudest possible volume to persuade the animal to de-couch, but the dog won't budge, not until it catches sight of me. Only then does it hop down and come to the side of my chair. However I might admire the dog for its taste in furniture or its indifference to the woman's tirade, I am compelled to stay put while the woman reviews the rules of animal ownership as they apply to her personal living quarters. I am able to do this without actually listening to the text of her rant, an ability acquired syndromatically or by dint of practice. At first her caviling screed parrots the histrionic harmonics preferred by the characters in her favorite teevee shows, the ones where enraged family members scream at one another about real or perceived slights to their well-being; the first source of her tutelage in such matters, but soon I detect something else, something in the unintended undertones of her nervous twittering, a plaintive, desperate, fragile mewling that draws me back into her words. Some certain though unnamed thing is coming undone and she is helpless to stop it. I listen to the phrases, *falling apart, can't hold together anymore*; a theme begins to emerge from behind her harangue about allergies and dog hair; that the dog's decamping in her living room is just one more act in a swirling cataclysm of events too complex for my understanding; because the Mexicans; because the increment remains unrealized; because the horses will not spit; because the lock was on the gate; because Otto has a secretary and a party has been planned and the goddamn cars and what money means and because despite all she's done, all she's done, all and more that she has personally done but Gustav will not get better. She's working herself into quite a froth. The dog and I listen politely, or we try. We could actually leave at any time. All the while she is pacing madly, the fancy rug muffling her clip clopping, and it seems to me that she's not really addressing me at all, her *why this* and *how come* no longer are subject to my reflexive response. She needs to talk. Sometimes it's all she needs. It is only when I hear the magic question: *Oh Gussie, what am I going to do?* in that all too familiar fix-it-for-me tone that I turn my chair and make for the back door.

You remember what I said, Gustav! Keep that mutt out of my house!

Parting words from the queen of caffeine.

SIXTEEN

From the increment festive waves of laughter and music wash up and down the face of the mountain like a search light. The dog and I make our escape out the laundry room and onto the drive by the ramp to the underground garage. It's wicked hot today, the sun beats down on us for all it's worth and commotion seems to be waiting for me wherever I turn. Never in the history of commotion has it ever been this bad. All at once, life on the side of the mountain is all over my nervous nerves. The desire to flee its hysterical inhabitants, the incessant yammering and Lilly's therapeutic machinations has reached a wearisome intensity. My head is beginning to throb with the sweltering heat. The dog is panting hard. The dumb nudge of urgency is upon me, but to where? Where is there a place for us? The thing is, the garage is cool and quiet. Never mind looking for Penzio. He's his own kind of commotion. If the two of us can just get down below and sit quietly for awhile all will be forgiven.

 The ramp. I contemplate its significant decline. Not in this chair, Gustav. My hands are its only brakes. I could easily lose control and hurtle down the steep slide with nothing between me and the big window. I'd plunge right through the glass and over the cliff, down down, so to begin my fossildom.

 Maybe there is a way. A tricky bit of piloting, to be sure. Keep a wheel against the edge of the curb and let friction slow me down. Yes, it can be done. I feel sure I can do this. I bring the left wheel of my chair to the edge of the ramp, snug it against the concrete curb and relax my grip. The dog lets out a bark. Now gravity, which is one of the few things that is what it is about and not about something else (I'd be surprised if gravity wasn't gravity at all but a heretofore unimagined thing like, say, a cosmic indifference to up), commands my forward and downward motion, and a much greater motion it is than I first anticipated, more powerful than these weary hands can manage. The plunge that I first considered a possibility is now taking place. As I zoom past the phalanx of furarrees (they all seem quite jealous of my speed), I'm glad the dog doesn't feel about the ramp the same way it feels about the elevator. It's robust barking is a fitting accompaniment to my predicament. I attempt to recapture my grip on the chair's wheels but with a single touch I realize the skin on my hands would come clean off were I try to stop myself at this point. It seems that I am at the bidding of the laws of physics and whatever luck might come my way. Moments before I hit the big window, the dog in hot pursuit (good dog, and yes, that's a very silly place to put a window), I think it is possible I am about to die and there are few thoughts more powerful than the fear of death unless that fear has been syndromatically disconnected from one's internal synapses, in which case the trepidation of ending is no more disturbing than the prospect of beginning. It's all about fundamental principles, and whatever atoms are all about. Or that one thing that is only about itself. How can a perfectly imperfect collection of atoms called Gustav Arturo Deal have any special claim on their use in this flicker of an instant called a lifetime? It seems such a broad and unsupportable conceit when those things that are not about other things need to move along, to be somewhere else and something else, the happenstance of my consciousness notwithstanding. I hope the dog doesn't feel obliged to go over the edge with me. After all, it just got here. The meals are regular and there's a fair sized yard to run about in. Nothing about being owned by a human demands the obligation of self-sacrifice. And sure, we've gotten along pretty well together so far for having just met, but it'll have other opportunities. It's a trained guard dog, after all, and if he doesn't stay on here with Otto and Lilly (although I don't see how that can work out since the man is not interested in it and the woman obviously fears it), well then I suppose it will find another house on another mountain with some fearful people who feel the need to be guarded. The potential is unlimited for that sort of thing, I imagine. It should anticipate a long life of barking at shadows in someone else's back yard if only it has the good sense not to take this plunge I myself am about to take in a matter of a milli....

It is Penzio's significant outstretched arm that arrests my forward motion and sends me smack to the seat of my pants on the hard marble floor. The chair slides out from under me and slams into the window with a thud, but the window does not break, not even a crack. Not glass after all.

I think you are too crazy, my friend, the mechanic says to me, kneeling over my prostrate self, and it occurs to me at that moment that I have never seen the underside of his mustache. The dog's massive head descends upon me as well and provides my face with an ample licking. With Penzio's help I manage to lift myself up on one arm and push the dog away. I'm alright, I think, just a little sore in the rump.

Penzio retrieves the chair which has not faired as well, a bent something or other has rendered it useless. He says, *Hey, I take you to where they watch the teevee. You sit there, okay?*

Yes, I tell him gratefully.

The mighty Italian lifts me up onto his back like I was no more than a sack of car parts. With the dog in tow, we cross the showroom floor to the scrum of nameless, non-priced furniture where they sometimes bring their guests to drink drinks and watch teevee. Penzio gingerly deposits me on the sofa so that I might lie on my side. The dog takes up a place by my head so that I can employ his significant self as a pillow. Friendly gestures, much appreciated.

You gave me a scare, Gustavo. You are a very lucky man I am here today because maybe I be here no more, I no tell you why, but I come back for some things and ekko! here comes Gustavo like capi-

tano Enzo and I grab you. One second too much and you are a big spot on the window. Stupeedo window. Yes, we are very lucky today.

He's sitting in one of Lilly's chairs with his dirty overalls. This strikes me as far more dangerous than what I just did.

Hey, you got a dog, eh? Datsa good. I have a dog once in my home. Best dog in all of Italy. Bella, I call her, because she was a beauty, like whadda you call it, catches the sheep, but she no catch the sheep cause I have no sheep, just dog. You okay, yes?

Yes, I tell him. I believe I am.

Datsa good. In my mind I see you go into that window and I think, God save Gustavo, but the dog, he save you. He's a good boy. A good pillow too. Dogs are no like people. Much better than people. My Bella, she was a good dog. When I leave Italy I miss her more than everyone. Penzio lights a cigarette and spends some time coughing. The dog lifts his head and pants. I ache all over now. Perhaps I'll sleep a bit. The room is dark and cool, just what I was looking for. I try to sit up and the dog stirs. Penzio has vanished. I have a headache. My legs are gone. I'm stuck on this sofa for awhile. Then I remember the tuna sandwich wrapped in the napkin in my pocket. The dog thinks it's very tasty.

When I was five, eons and epochs ago, there was no house on the side of the mountain, no fancy cars or stiff-necked chef from France or anywhere else, and no wheelchair. I was a running boy and a climber, an intrepid explorer of new worlds, a fearless adventurer. I would leap through the branches of a tree like a giddy chimpanzee and I would not be contained. Were there friendly children to companion me through the jungles and thickets of that other world? I can see only their shadows now, faceless, nameless little creatures alit on a caravan of bicycles. The neighborhood for us was the Universe as far as we could roam. I remember play. It was serious business and much was invested in its proper execution. The rules of the game obsessed us. Did we laugh? I hope we laughed enough.

When I stopped running I remember a room and a simple bed with a brown woolen blanket, and next to the bed a table and a lamp and some books. The room had a single window with a wide ledge where I often perched to watch the flurry of life that occupied the tree whose branches were just out of reach. And more than once I was scolded off that favorite spot by a woman who vaguely resembles the woman who presently occupies the scene, exhorting, pleading, get down, get away, too dangerous. I remember that hysterical voice. She had no idea what a world class brachiator I had once been.

That was then, another era. Beyond all that, those tiny scraps, the pictures stop, the teevee fades to black. Perhaps the syndromes were upon me then, scrubbing the slate clean, wiping the words away, scrambling all the letters and numbers into nonsensical squiggles and rendering the books so much pointless clutter. Did I ever speak? Surely I had a voice once, a voice of my own that I commanded, a strong voice. I don't recall. The yes and no that comes popping out of me now sometimes feels like a vestigial appendage, an ancient tail attached to a failed hominid, and I sense that I must have once used those words purposefully, to make choices, to take positions and state objections, instead of what yes and no mean now, an accommodation I make to others against my will. And if it should turn out that I never speak again, I would choose to be rid of these last remnants of speech as they do not befit my spirit. If all goes well, I'd like to move beyond yes and no to something more agreeable to me, perhaps a solid, reliable grunt. And couple that with the slightly inscrutable hmm, the one sound that seems to mean everything. How about barking? I could bark. That's not so bad, is it Dog? Wake the neighbors in the middle of the night. What's wrong with that? I'll bet your furry head spins with all those sounds the humans make, those pointy consonants and slippery vowels, slushes and clacks, half spitting sputzes and breathy whohowwhos. You can't imagine the chaos and grief and unutterable confusion all those noises cause people. Peaceful fellow you must be. What would you say if you could? If you could deliver just one line, what would it be? I know what you'd say. You'd tell them: Stop. Sit. Stay. Now think about what you've done.

Dog and I sit on the sofa together in the dark looking out the big window as the day gives way to evening, and maybe both of us are thinking about barking or maybe we're not thinking about anything at all, just sitting when the light from the elevator spreads through the garage.

I expected Penzio, but it is Lilly who emerges from the little golden car pushing another chair for me. She comes more or less rushing up to me while asking in her best motherly voice, *Gussie, honey, are you okay?*

Yes, I tell her.

Yes? Really yes?

Yes, I say. It so happens that I am.

Penzio said you fell. You went down the ramp again, didn't' you?

No.

No. Yes. No. Yes. I don' t know what I'd do if anything happened to you.

Despite this display of mushgush and the pained look on her face, the woman does not approach as the dog is sitting up beside me, on one of her sofas no less, and giving her a good stare down.

Really, Gustav. What am I going to do?

There it is again and I'm trapped. She specializes in all things exasperated.

I'm so tired of it all, the lies, the deceptions. Why must it be this way?

Heal thyself, woman, I would tell her.

I brought you a chair. The electric one is still charging. This is the last spare so take care of it. Lilly takes the seat farthest from the dog and begins the well-practiced ritual of wringing the hands and rubbing the temples.

It's all too much, too much. You have no idea what's going on. I think I just might lose my mind. You should be glad you can't under-stand things, and catching herself, *Oh honey, I don't mean you should be...you know. Hell, I'm all discombobled. Your father has made a real mess of it this time, that crappy business of his, don't get me started.*

That's the last thing I would want to do.

I'm really afraid. Afraid of what's happening to us, what's happening to you. Oh, I wish we could get you better. If you would just get better I think I could cope. Gussie, you know I love you.

Now there's a phrase that spells trouble.

Things may change. I don't know how or when but things are going to be different. Promise me you'll understand. No matter what happens I want you to know that you'll always have a mother who loves you. Do you understand?

Yes, I say.

And do you love me?

Yes, I tell her.

It's a waxy, unsatisfied smile she gives me, always knowing what I'll say. She takes a hankie from the pocket of her floppy shirt and wipes her eyes.

Of course you do. My brave little man. I wish I had your strength.

If I could speak right now I would say nothing.

The woman gathers herself and rises. *Well, things will work out. They always do, don't they?*

No.

I mean they won't, will they?

Yes.

Oh Christ, I can never get that right. You know what I mean. Now listen, I want you to go back to your little house and stay there. Your father is having some people over this evening for a business meeting upstairs. Maybe they'll figure something out. I'll have chef bring you a nice plate of spaghetti. So take your dog and go, okay?

Yes, I tell her.

Be happy to.

And Gussie, mommy will always be mommy, no matter what. And I won't give up until you're my smart handsome son again. We'll find a way together, like we always do. Now go.

Lilly crosses the concourse of cars and takes the ride up the elevator and out of sight. The dog is panting heavily and I'm sure I know how he feels. I could use a drink of water myself right about now.

SEVENTEEN

The chair Lilly delivered is only minimally a working device. The seatback is way out of kilter with the seatseat and, weirdly, both wheels. The one armrest is wobbly loose and the footrests are completely cockeyed. I wheel myself forward to see how it handles...not so bad, better than it looks like it should. I'll turn it a bit this way...easy enough, that's good...and that way...whoa, donkey! No right. I've got no right turn. The wheels go forward but when I attempt to turn right the thing seizes up. The mechanic will have to explain that one to me. In the meantime, full circles to the left will get me right. There's a solution to every problem.

Hmm, I think. I have another problem. How to get Dog out of the garage. The elevator is out the question. No going up the ramp, not in this thing. Not in my battered condition. I give Dog a quizzical expression, but all I get from him is a furry face. There's something to envy in that.

His ears bristle, then I too hear a bump in the dark. Around the corner comes Penzio, ever so slightly skulking.

Gustavo, shhhh. Hey, thatsa funny, eh? I tell you to shhhh. But for sure, Gustavo, no make noise because I am hiding, I no tell you why.

I think Penzio has sized up the situation.

The dog, he no like the elevator. Smart dog. I tell you what we do.

You go up, and the dog and I we use the ramp and meet you at your little house. That's a plan, eh?

Yes, I tell him. That's a good plan.

The dog is also responsive to the idea and goes bounding off with Penzio.

Up on the main floor the waitress and the French chef are engaged in the kind of frenetic flitting about from kitchen to dining room and beyond that can only mean that we are truly on the verge of a massive influx. Lilly appears on the scene, fully ornamented, red uniformed and no less frenetic herself.

Go home, I said. Right this minute. Please!

I prefer to leave. No please required. In fact, I consider it good advice. Certainly I will go. I should go. Why even think of sticking around? I'm hungry, tired and thoroughly banged up. There's nothing to see here save Otto and his business buddies yammering about money all night, with Otto as chief yammerer, the vice president of yawking. The head pounds at the thought. Yet, if I were to stay, and for only the briefest interval, an on-the-way-out-the-door kind of peek, it would be with the intention of discovering what the hell is going on around here. There's no getting past it; something is definitely up on the side of the mountain. Its ferocious occupants are loosed with fear and there's no telling what cranky unkindnesses they are scheming to unleash. Tremble I would—were I the trembling kind—at the advent of their well-practiced misbehavior. These are dangerous times; the words of a windbag, yes, but not without some merit. I have no desire to be a soldier in whatever self-aggrandizing crusade they are plotting, specialist gardener second class reporting for sacrifice. My interest is not getting caught in the crossfire. There's no glory, Mr. Vice President, in being among the collaterally damaged.

But I can't stay here. The main dining room will serve as the evening's theater of operations, the goddamn dining room, as Otto calls it, where only glum holiday meals with Otto's sisters and their glum mates take place. The waitress skitters by in search of a crooked fork, or so I think; it appears that she is going from place to place turning all the silverware askew. Ah, perfidy's afoot alright.

The dining room table, stately oak unceremoniously felled, is all dressed and ready for battle. Gold-throated plates and resolute candlesticks. Ardent white napkins folded fancy bivouac style. The full deployment of crystal goblets. Makes my arm twitch just to think about it. And backlighting provided by the malfunctioning Lady of the Infanticidal Clamshell taking her usual place at the head of the table. Wheeling myself out of harm's way proves somewhat problematic as the most direct path of retreat requires more than one of the newly inconvenient left turns and I manage to down only a single piece of silly glass thing the woman insists on keeping in my way. With my last turn I almost hit the Argentinean waitress—I know her well enough now to know when she is being Argentinean.

Seenyour Gustav, you must go now, she babbles. Pull yourselves together, dear. I'm leaving. And right behind her the French chef adds, *Wee, wee, ma damn mommy says shoo.* What am I supposed to make of that?

There is, owing to the castle's abundance of pointless architecture, one place I can hide out, to spy, as it were, if the truth be told. I never spy, and this is owing to an otherwise complete indifference on my part to the activities of the man and the woman. I will admit to myself that I am somewhat intrigued by this new idea, being an observer by nature and disposition, though not a curious observer of people particularly; people are too screwed up. I don't know what's the matter with them.

The site I've chosen for my obscuration is the library, located upstairs and directly above the dining room. I manage to make my way to the elevator without contacting anymore of the woman's inane collection of breakables, and on the trip up I catch a view of the driveway full of headlights (they'll all be obliged to view the real view before it's all over tonight). The library door is ridiculously large and creaks when I open it. Not a good noise for a spy to make. I locate my intended perch. There may be a good reason why a balcony was installed in the library overlooking the dining room—so that hungry readers and bored diners might toss one another some relief—but for the purpose of covert surveillance it is ideal. I adjust the shutters to provide the maximum viewing angle with the minimum degree of exoposure, then I wait.

The visitors are taking their time. I imagine all the flesh pressing, back slapping, phony guffawing has got them thoroughly occupied, probably on the patio gawking at infinity in the dark and asking about the kids. No one will be coming this way, to be sure. This is not a house of readers. I don't remember ever seeing a book in Lilly's hand and Otto reads only single sheets of paper. Nevertheless, an entire wall in this dour room is lined with fancy carved bookshelves which are loaded with crumbly old books that Lilly bought from the same place she bought the chairs. A display for the public, nothing more. I don't like coming up here. It says to me that I must have been able to read once upon a time. There are thing I know about that I could only have learned about from books. A child reading? A man? This library is nothing more than a Potemkin village. And how would I know about that? A conversation overheard at breakfast? Who do you think you're fooling with this pathetic display, Lilly...mother, if that's who you really are? Nothing about you is about what it's about, is it? Do you think you're kidding me with this clumsy show, your moron son, the retard, the mental defective. I see everything So why won't you tell what happened to me that I should be this way, that I should be here in this room with these books and not be able to open a single one and decipher its meaning, or to stare at what I know to be words and see only squiggles and swirls in between the punctuation like so much Chinese? What happened to me, Lillian? Why can't I remember? A person should be able to remember. A person should know the truth. That's what these books are about, aren't they, somebody trying their damnedest to know the truth? The famous truth? Some things can't be covered up with fancy.

Voices begin to fill the house signaling the arrival of Otto's business bund. The lights have been dimmed to a gloomy glow. A somber, blue-suited bunch file into the dining room, tall, short, fat, skinny, bald and otherwise. Some seem too young for their clothes, while for others their cheerless costumes fit just right. The voices are reduced to whispers as the men take their seats. The chair at the head of the table remains dramatically vacant. An interval passes and the whispers become silence. A familiar clip clop is heard. Lilly enters the room. All men rise.

Lilly: Please be seated, gentleman. In a moment you will joined by the president of our company, Mr. Otto Deal. He has asked you here this evening to discuss an important matter of importance to us all. (She stops momentarily to whisper at a column) After Mr. Deal finishes concluding his remarks (more, snappy whispering) a light supper and coffee will be served. So without further to do, here he is, the boss, Otto Deal.

Lilly turns and engages in some more argue whispering with the marble column. When she clip clops off, Otto emerges in the wake of Lilly's mangled intro. Applause greets him as he marches the length of the table to his place at the helm, his phone hand wrapped in a dirty handkerchief.

For a long time he says nothing and everyone waits in silence. Standing by the window, Otto sees what I hear; the rumble of Lilly's car heading down the drive. At that point Otto turns to his guests.

Otto: Thank you, gentleman. I asked you here this evening to discuss the subject of our mutual prosperity, which is to say, your reliance on me. Certain sudden and unforeseen changes in the economic climate of our times now threaten to undermine our valiant enterprise, changes profound as they are inconvenient, and yet there are those who would deny the facts and dismiss the evidence of this assault on our advantage as nothing more than a momentary shift in the trade winds, and no cause for alarm. I have become aware that one of you has taken this position and are engaged in spreading your reckless incredulity to your subordinates. This must stop...

...It occurs to me that the health of our endeavor, which is to say my own salutary outlook, depends upon a more thorough understanding by those who would call themselves my lieutenants of their commander's resume. After all, we work together, make money together, and it's been good, has it not? (The men in suits murmur their assent). But such an endeavor cannot take place in a vacuum with the knowns and unknowns of the more intimate details of my personal profile the scurrilous subject of water cooler speculation. Gossip, gentlemen, is labor of fools and naysayers who bear unwanted cargo aboard this ship. However, I am prepared to concede that some of you may be innocent in your ignorance, having only recently boarded our intrepid vessel, and the goals of our mission may lodge confused in your minds, the unfortunate result of an incomplete understanding of the essential nature of its author. To that end, I shall speak tonight upon a singular topic and pose a fundamental question, to wit, who is Otto Deal?...

...I am Otto the Owl, gentleman. I have the ears of an owl and the eyes of a night stalker. I kill with my beak, my deadly beak, the little bitty mice. The bittier the better. Bitty babies are the best. Better than all the rest. And see how they run. Run, babies, run. Run to Otto. Get rich the Otto the Owl way. Learn all the secrets of the Real Deal Method and in no time at all you'll be on the road to riches. That's what we tell them, isn't it? More money than their mice minds can possibly imagine; fancy cars, big houses, blow their little mouse noses with hundred dollar bills. Oh, those tails go awaggin', don't they? Those bitty whiskers quiver, they can hardly wait. But how much, O Otto, they ask? How much will it cost us to be just like you? O Mousey, I can taste you now. The key to your fortune, my scrumptious nibble, is only three easy payments of nineteen ninety-five, because I know you're always good for a twenty. And then I say...and I love this part... I say, But wait! If you call in the next five seconds the mice are stupid method can be yours for a special mice price of only two payments! That's right, my darlings. I'll make those payments for you, just give old Otto all those numbers on your little plastic cards and Otto will make those payments, the first and second and fourth and seventh and as many as I like. Why so many, they ask? Because I can. Because they didn't read the fine mice print. Because they'll never find me. Because mice don't hunt owls...

...Yes, petite ones, you'll get your lessons, all right, once a month for eternity. Second class mail. And let's say you don't become fabulously wealthy overnight. Say you remain a total failure and a complete asswipe. Say you still feel miserable about yourself and your worthless mouse existence. How come, you say! Why can't I be one of the pretty people, O Otto? This dilemma weighs heavily on your tiny mouse minds. In your aimless wanderings maybe you see a magazine at the checkout line where you buy your beer and cigarettes, and it's full of pictures of the so-called pretty people. But they're not so pretty, you think. Your beady eyes scan the pages of bloated starlets in bikinis fighting with their liquor sodden boyfriends on some fancy French beach, and Geez, you squeak! How hard can it be? You start to get all hopeful again so your read on. And there, towards the back cover, just waiting for you, the classified ads. Two glorious pages of razzmatazz devoted to your every personal development fantasy. Row upon row of single syllable doubletalk, facile fixes, fake remedies, phony restitutions and rehabilitations. Lose Fifty Pounds Eating All you Want!..Overcome Any Addiction in One Day!..Teach Yourself Party Piano!..Yell Your Way to Winning Arguments!..Ha! Any silly thing we can think of. They buy them by the mailbag full. Regain Your Vigor in the Bedroom, a Handbook!..Foolproof Lucky Coin, shipping and handling extra!...Ha! Vitamins You Smoke!..A Special Message from Jesus Just for You!..Ha! Secrets to a Swarthy Complexion!..Best Ever Lamp Chop Recipes!..Ha! Ha! And all brought to you by none other than Otto the Owl. A cavalcade of hope for the damned. Hope against hope for the helpless, the sick of spirit, the lame of heart. Life's cruelties cured! All for just the low low price. Satisfaction guaranteed. Cash only. Sorry, no refunds...

...This, gentlemen, is the course upon which I steer; navigator, captain and master. I have but one destination in sight: limitless wealth. You are my crew. You have but one duty to perform: the exercise of unwavering loyalty to me. I will tolerate nothing less. Unhappily, gentlemen, one of you has failed to understand this. So we ask ourselves, what is it that would make a man question his duty? What would compel this man to upend our prosperous voyaging? Upon what principles could this betrayal reside? It is clear to us that this man must know nothing of our own journey to this time and place or the perils which schooled us to our station as your skipper, the adversities we stared down, the tribulations that sharpened our sight and strengthened our resolve. If this man is among us tonight, and I know that he is, then he must be as ignorant of the past as he is of the present, that he would dare to engage us in battle, for this is a fight I have fought all my life. I am bred to this fight. I welcome this fight. I shall not be undone by heathens and naysayers, regardless of stripe.

Let us begin then with a poem of my own device. It is entitled Song of Me, and I shall declaim it forthwith.

> Do we know who did this thing to us?
> Upon what villain, scoundrel, knave shall
>   the onus
> Fall? Drunkards, cretins, the lords of
>   noblesse,
> Permissive parents, freedom of the press?
> Do we know for sure, do we have any idea?
> Shall we detain the King of North Korea?
> Put him on the rack and spit
> And grill him in the fire pit?
> Or ought we ply him with gin and sweet
>   vermouth
> Until he volunteers for us the famous truth,
> But truth is not our final goal my friends,
> Hardly is it a beginning, never is it an end.
> For what we seek and why we came
> Begs the question, who among you will
>   catch the blame?
>
> Let us return by flight of mind and
>   contemplation,
> Speak memory, the morn of my
>   perturbation,
> A sunny day to be sure; eggs, coffee, a little
>   teevee,

A birthday gift for boy, a car, that he
May one day detach from the weakened
    kind
And join us speech restored and right
    of mind.
Yet my scheme for boy drew no consensus
From my darling nosy little missus,
Not so little, granted, quite broad in
    the beam
She is, and whatever kind of honey she
    may seem,
That nose costs more than three of you,
Salaries, bonuses and Blue Cross too.
By the way, when comes time for truth's
    decree,
I shall reveal who of you Lilly's boyfriend
    be.

But let us stick to the topic on the table.
My dilemma was grander than a jumper
    cable
Applied to the antipode of my Mercedes
    Benz.
We're talking loss of liberty and all that that
    portends.
Upon the iron gate a lock was placed that
    we may not be free,
Not freedom of this or freedom from that
    but freedom without degree.
I count myself a patriot, an abider of the law,
A shameless love of liberty is not my tragic
    flaw.
In the shade of arboreal splendor that is
    my drive,
I sought the meaning of what is it to
    be alive.

DOG CHRIST

I sought and thought and caught a particular
    view
Of what a man like me does, and what
    others do.
Shall I wish them well, of thee I sing?
Then let me first ask them, who do
    this thing?

Upon this very gate, my home, my castle,
    who dares intrude?
Who concocts such infamy then eats
    my food?
A calumny played out upon our noble rank,
Designed for what purpose, to break
    the bank?
Or send our soul to depths of morbid
    desperation,
Without regard for our special station,
That spins a cloth for the general good,
And by general I mean the neighborhood.
Those like of mind and will, the chosen ilk,
Who deign to boil a kid in its mother's milk.
Whose genius for profit is deemed a
    covetous fate
By those who would put a lock upon
    our gate.
And curse that money flows in a downward
    direction
As if the law of gravity were our invention.

My heart is heavy with grief and despair.
For those who would love us I no longer
    care.
The timid, the weak, the poor of sight,
They squeal like mice for their civil right.
And snivel discontent of a puny hue

Because they lack my commanding view.
This is my mountain! my stone house!
God damn the imputation of the mouse!
I am Otto the Owl, by night I stalk,
The eyes of a killer, the beak of a hawk.
Save your pouty querulous questions,
The rights of mice give me indigestion.
Don't give me your mushy sophistry,
I know my poem is lovelier than a tree.

I remember my father, a soldier once,
Who fought for them, out of obedience.
But not upon the battlefield,
A personal weapon he would not wield.
He didn't care for fighting much;
Instead he made the bombs and gas
    and such
In a factory of his own commencement
Though just a lad, he showed a penchant
For making silk purses from the sow's ear.
An entrepreneur, though some cried
    profiteer
And after the war the righteous mice
    objected
To the riches this clever boy collected.
They took his money and closed his shop
And led him in chains to the judge's stop.

A life behind bars? No coward he.
When chance came calling he decided
    to flee
Beneath the offal of the garbage truck
And off to Switzerland, with a little luck.
From there to France, then to Italy
Where he met Mom and they had me.
Then off again, to Argentina,

The three of us and new sister Gina.
Was life there good? I couldn't say.
I was but a babe when they gave us away
To an aunt in Pennsylvania who taught us
    both to speak.
Say Ma, say Pa...such was her tried and true
    technique,
Having practiced on her own babes not long
    before;
Say run, fetch, dig, and be sure you close the
    cellar door.

Good people. Yes, good people or good
    enough.
The woman was cranky, the man was rough.
They believed in work, country, food
    and Jesus
And insisted we avoid those things that
    pleased us
Like play and toys and riding a bike;
It's the devil's work, those things we like.
But Gina and I were always fed.
Come nine o'clock we were off to bed.
There were chores to do and prayers to say;
By sixteen years old I had exhausted
    my stay.
I left my dear sister alone in that house
With half sister Doris and half brother
    Klaus
To learn the world and the secrets it might
    reveal,
Not with my own name but as Otto Deal.

The road was hard and long, my struggle
    great,
I slept in bus stations and hardly ate

A decent meal unless some poor sot loosed
    a fin
My way by dint of pity or to his chagrin,
I took it anyway from its pocket hold.
One learns the cunning theft when nights
    are cold,
When hunger and fear grip a boy on
    the run,
And the end seemed upon me though I'd
    hardly begun.
It was on the eve of the last day in
    December,
In the freezing privy of a filling station and I
    remember
I was not alone and at it, the most shameful
    dollar,
When I pondered the test of my genuine
    father
And resolved by God if he loved me indeed,
That I'd gain my fortune, this slave would
    be freed!

I set my direction south to a warmer clime.
I took what I wanted which meant I
    did time
In the county clink more than once, but
    uncontained
Was my heart for I dreamed a dream
    unrestrained
By a commoner's conditions for honest play.
No sappy morality tale would bar my way
Up the mountain, and when my sojourn I
    did reach,
I took up residence upon the sunny beach
Of the Floridian shore to rest and
    contemplate

DOG CHRIST

A plan of attack that I could activate
By sheer power of will and strength of spirit,
But after a month or so I was no closer to it,
And found myself, lo, once again
For an extended stay in the jailer's pen.

There's not much to tell about the interval,
Between then and freedom was no festival.
I brushed my teeth and made my bed.
I don't recall all the books I read.
Much later, unchained, I worked the streets
And learned the wisdom of the Miami
    cheats
To win a buck or two or three.
It was through this magic I would be free
In time. It came to me as no surprise
That I had found a worthy enterprise.
T'was the hawker's game I did excel,
Watches, trinkets, nothing, nothing! I could
    not sell.
Used up cars, a wireless phone,
I sold a house I did not own.

And bought another, a modest retreat,
On a desperate, troubled, palm lined
    street,
Where demand was high for a soothing
    tonic,
Some called it bliss, some called it chronic.
The fateless, broken and weary of life,
Bullied and beaten by the common strife,
Sought their release with dollars in hand,
A shabby lot, beneath contempt. I bought
    some land
With my easy winnings, sold it quickly and
    got some more,

Then chased forever that sulky sodden
    traffic from my door.
Nevermore. From there on in I would
    go legit,
Get married, go west and start anew; I
    must admit
None to soon, for the law was making things
    chilly
For me and my silly filly Lilly.

I came to this desert a score and some ago;
Nobody special, just a regular Joe,
With some cash, a wife and one thought
    alone,
How to get rich with a telephone.
Now many of you might find it enlightening
To learn how I forked telephonic lightning...

EIGHTEEN

Rhyming couplets, the poor poet's plowhorse. And he's tilling me under. I can't listen to another word. I fall asleep and the dimmest of dreams begins to emerge from blissful nothingness.

A street. Houses, crowded up one side down the other. Roofs and driveways. Old cars loiter at the curb. The sun is blazing hot, the pavement quivers. Not a tree in sight. I am walking down the street. Maybe I am looking for something, maybe not. One house looks familiar so I follow the walkway to the front door. The screen is torn, the button on the doorbell is missing. I think I might knock, but I don't. Instead I follow the plain stone path to a carless carport cluttered with dusty boxes, old bicycles and folding lawn chairs. The path continues around back, but the way is blocked by a rusty fence with a gate and a chain. A padlock dangles from the chain, undone. I snap the lock shut. There's another door and I enter the house. I am in a tiny room with a single bed, and a woman is trying to shove something under the mattress. I have to help her because there's someone in the bed who can't move. I am in the kitchen, the man and the woman are sitting at a table drinking coffee, the sink is full of dirty dishes. I look at my reflection in the silver coffee pot, my nose is enormous. I am on the back patio which is covered with a mat of plastic grass. There's an old, weather beaten metal table with a torn umbrella off to one side by a greasy barbeque. I look out over the yard, dead lawn and weeds surrounded by a block wall. A tangled hose lies unconnected to a dripping faucet. At the far end I see a tree and I run to it, but it's not a tree at all, just a bush that looks like a tree, much too small to climb. Now I am in the carport with stacks of boxes marked Kitchen and Bedroom. I brush up against one, it falls, and out spills some papers with writing and numbers on them, also a photograph of a boy in a uniform that's too big, the sleeves come down over his hands. I am on the patio and there's a tree in the yard and I run to it, but its not a tree just a dead stick in the ground. Someone yells Get down! and I trip and fall, there's a horrific crack. And I am driving a car down the street, a real piece of shit, the top is down, one hand on the wheel, feeling the wind in my hair. I take a drag from my cigarette and turn up the radio, they're playing that song I like about how bad I am. So I hit the gas and the engine coughs, the road turns steep and there's some old fucker in my way. I give him the horn and pull along side. He yells, Hey! so I cut him right off and yell Fuck off! back at him or at no one in particular. And I am in the bedroom and the woman is trying to lift the mattress but it's too heavy, someone is sick. I lift it for her, she stuffs a handful of money underneath. The woman is crying, her makeup is running down her cheeks, her eyes are red and swollen. She wraps her head in a cloth so I won't see her tears. And I am driving a car down the street, where the Mexicans live, roofs and driveways, the Mexicans see me and come out of their houses to wave and yell Hey Zeus be praised moo-chacho! I take a long sweet swig of beer and turn up that song I like about how bad I am, O Haupt voll Blut und Wunden, and suddenly I see that the world is all roofs and driveways after all, and all the yards have fountains with mothers on the half shell; your babies are drowning, ladies...What's that in your hand? Show me. What are you holding? Let me see it, NOW, I yell Jesus Fucking Christ! I am running. I fall. There's a horrific crack. I want to tell them. Not this, I say. No more of this. I am standing in the yard by a stump where a tree used to be.

NINETEEN

I shake myself awake. It's getting light and Otto is still at it. Something about a real deal and how mice are stupid. I can't listen to business talk anymore, and besides, the smell of stale cigar smoke is turning my stomach. I think about Dog outside alone. Maybe he left. Maybe he went to look for me and got lost. I'm going to find him right now.

    Dog is lying in the doorway of the shack. He seems glad to see me. We sit quietly on the porch together and watch the sun come up. The birds in the trees with their nervous twittering are the first creatures to stir at daybreak. Next, the Mexicans, no less nervous with all the sounds children make and the scurrying to start the day. A fire is lit on the top floor of the increment, the women are busy preparing the morning meal. The smell of searing flesh fills the air and between the two of us only Dog appreciates this. His nose is very attentive. In the distance Lilly is stepping on to the east patio and taking her place at the enormous glass top table, all by herself.

    Two young Mexican boys from the increment are in the yard throwing a tennis ball back and forth. The grass hasn't been mowed for awhile, and when one of the boys drops the ball it disappears into the thick rough. Dog watches every throw with great interest. When one of the boy's overthrows his companion's reach the ball lands near the porch, and Dog leaps up, snatches the ball and steals it away to the tennis court. The boys protest and run after him. I wonder what Dog has in mind. He's much larger than these boys, significantly so, and he's purported to be a trained guard dog. I assume he is also a trained attack dog—isn't that what guard dogs do? Should I be concerned? The boys don't seem to be too worried. They chase Dog, but Dog isn't ready to give up his prize and he starts to run too, dodging their best efforts to retrieve their toy. Dog dares the boys to catch him, and I realize that my lumbering giant is enjoying a keep-away game he and his new found playmates have spontaneously devised. The boys are giving Dog a good run, round and round the net which has somehow become central to the game, the rules known only to three of them. They seem to be inexhaustible running back and forth, the boys laughing and screaming their arcane commands, the dog ignoring them and darting wildly from their grasp. Finally, Dog is obliged to take a rest. The boys catch up as he flops on the fake green grass. Amazingly, one of the boys just reaches into Dog's great maw and snatches the ball away. Dog immediately springs back up. Again I become concerned. That boy seems so small beside my rough beast. What might Dog do to regain the ball? It would be nothing for him to overpower the child, a single flouncing of his significant paw and the boy would be helpless. Could I stop it?

    Quickly I wheel myself down to the edge of the court hoping my presence alone will deter Dog from some brutish instinctual reaction. The boy waves the ball in front of Dog's face, teasing him with it, trying to get him to react in some way. But by all accounts the game is still on and Dog knows what he must do. Assuming an altogether steely sit position, he waits, head transfixed to the motion of the ball in the boy's hand, to and fro, the boy's arm moves in a long sweeping arc, ever more deliberate. Then, all at once, the boy tosses the ball across the tennis court. Dog dashes after it, a mass of black fur in singular pursuit, the boys squealing their encouragements. The ball travels the length of the court, bounces off the wall, and Dog, in one glorious leap, snatches it midair to the hooping and clapping of the boys. I find myself clapping too, though clapping is not a usual practice for me, but I cannot be contained. Surely, I don't know the rules of this game, for Dog then trots right back to his playmates and delivers the ball at their feet. So much I do not understand. Immediately, the boy grabs the ball and gives it another toss, and off goes Dog again, obtaining the weak throw this time before it hits the wall. And once more, he returns and relinquishes the ball, and prepares himself for another go. It's the other boy's turn to throw the ball now. He gives it a mighty launch in the air, more up than out, so that when the ball lands it takes a terrific bounce. I hold my breath...run, I think...get down, but the dog hurls himself upward, as if taking flight, extending his enormous body in full and for an instant he is suspended in space motionless, as if time itself would stop, before plucking from the air the descending orb in his massive jaws. It is a magnificent sight.

For Dog and his boys it is just part of the game and the game goes on. For me, I feel something completely unfamiliar; a faint laugh trickles across my lips.

TWENTY

Lilly has given up trying to chase the Mexicans from the increment. Instead, she has decided to become their victim and to bear the occupation of her house, albeit the incomplete and uninhabitable portion thereof, as a personal trial and tribulation, which she is exceedingly adept at doing. For their part, the Mexicans have ceased performing their landscaping chores as the main component of protest in whatever beef they have with the woman. If this is about money, which of course it must be, I am unaware of it. I only know what I see: the mowers are silent, the bushes are unclipped, the drive and walkways are littered with unblown debris. The place is looking more than a little seedy lately, but it doesn't take long. Turn your back on a rosebush for just a moment and it withers in despair. Also, the crew that comes to clean the pool and the fountains has been conspicuously absent. If I am not mistaken—from this distance and with my imperfect eyesight it is difficult to be sure—but I believe that's the French chef with a pole in his hands vacuuming the pool, and a question comes to mind; is it possible to do that job without turning the head?

I prepare myself a cheese and cracker breakfast from the small store of edibles I keep in my personal larder. Dog and I share this morning repast on the porch where the potting table serves as adequate a dining surface as any slab of glass. Dog's regard for cheese is unquestionable. I imagine every bite makes his eyes light up and sparkle, if I only I could see his eyes. He is, after all, fur, nose and tongue exclusively.

One of the Mexican men brings me some food on a paper plate. *Para oosted, seenyour.* I nod politely. A halfway decent gesture. Nothing to get churlish about. But the food is nothing I would eat, and when the man is out of sight I put the plate down on the ground for Dog. In a flash not even the plate remains. It must be liberating not to be a picky eater.

Despite the obvious deviations, the French chef cleaning the pool, the large and growing population of Mexicans residing in the half-realized shell that is the rear of the house, and Otto, who is now leading his exhausted employees around the yard like school children on a field trip to the zoo while rhyming the totality of his personal profile for their beleaguered edification, all is unfolding as it should on the side of the mountain at the house built entirely of stone. I admit to a restored sense of serenity following the many assaults against it since the singing of happy birthday. Could it be that the woman has exhausted her therapeutic bag of tricks and, as with the Mexicans, has chosen to suffer the burden of my syndromatic self and carry on, to endure, to engage in that most challenging of human activities, to cope? Is it conceivable that she has given up on the grand project, the one big thing that is at the very core of her existence, happiness? —to her that one thing that is about what it is about but is in fact about nothing at all. I think it unlikely. The woman is all about happiness. More than anything she wants to be happy, which is impossible because for her happiness will always mean not this but that, the elusive abstraction of satisfaction that promises to materialize tomorrow or the next day or the next. The word itself is like a cage, poor Lilly, she's caught in a cage fashioned from the utterance of some sounds in her throat and she's spared its meaning which happens to be the opposite of meaning, an empty and desperate utterance, a thing always out reach, absurd horizons out of focus, a mirage twisting its crazy dance on the desert when viewing the view. Happiness is a game without rules that I will not play. It's serenity I'm after. Peace of mind, in here, where I reside.

But then I hear Lilly clopping her way up the sidewalk and immediately I feel the sensation slipping away. She has that look about her. Something is going to happen, and I will not care a wit for it.

Gussie lamb, she warbles, stepping on to the porch. *Gussie, I'm taking you for a ride today. It'll be nice, honey. Really. We'll go visiting. You'll like that, sweetie.*

It's all peaks and valleys around here, peaks and valleys.

Come now. I want you to get cleaned up. Go take a shower and put on some clean clothes. I'll send the girl over with your new shirt all ironed and pretty. Hurry up then. And shave, honey, hear me? Mommy wants you to shave today.

In one perfectly imperfect moment I have been stripped of my serene sensation, and in its place I am promised a clean shirt and the prospect of being someone's...I can hardly allow myself to think it...company. Pointless to resist. It would take a seizure of epic proportions to get out of this one. Suddenly the incident at the ramp seems like a luckless event.

Removing my clothes is trial and tribulation enough for me right now. I'd rather take a nap. Dog watches the tugging and pulling with great interest. If I didn't know better I'd say he was laughing at me, but then why not, he doesn't have to go.

I usually transfer myself to the plastic bench when riding the electric but I figure there's little damage a quick shower could do to old lefty here, so I adjust the water temperature and wheel myself under the spray. I freely confess, there's nothing wrong with a cool shower on a hot summer day. I lather up, shut my eyes, and enjoy the sensation.

There was no knock at the door, I'm sure of that, and only the briefest of breezes that leads me to realize the door has been opened. Half blinded by shampoo lather, I can make out in the whitish blur a vaguely human figure and in an instant I am no longer alone.

Yer momma sent me along to help get yuz all prettied up for yer little outin'. You don't mind if I step in here with ya and give ya some good scrubbin', do ya darlin'?

She isn't really asking. It's the waitress in non-argentine mode. She is in the shower with me and altogether naked. This couldn't be what Lilly had in mind.

I though maybe ya could use some special attention, can't do no harm by my reckonin'. A little soapin' up might just be what ya been missin'.

I feel her small hands on my chest, across my shoulders.

Now ya can't tell me that doesn't feel good, baby, cause all ya gotta do is say so and I'll stop.

Her hand touches my leg, against my face I feel the press of softer flesh as she bends over me.

Say, this could get kinda interestin', she says in my ear. *But first I want to do somethin' about this mop a hair of yers, and these scraggly old whiskers too.*

I feel a comb's teeth pulling through my hair. The snip of a scissors.

Bet ya never yer hair cut in the shower before. I ain't gonna take but a touch off. I like a man with long wavy hair. Make ya look, I dunno, sorta biblical. What's them men in the bible ain't got no shaved heads, I'll bet. How's they gonna shave 'em anyway? They ain't got no razors, ain't been invented yet, had they? Course all those apostles and all had long hair and beards just like you. Why, Jesus Christ our lord in heaven, musta got himself some mighty pretty locks...turn yer head a might for me, will ya hon, yea, that's good. Ya can't imagine how nice it is to be with a man that can turn his head. Don't know what's a matter with that Jock and his head not turnin'. Don't think there's nothin' a matter with him, if ya wanna know the truth. Just don't want to be turnin' his head, that's all. I think that's kinda weird, don't you? I mean, a person not turnin' their head, just cause they don't feel like it. What's that all about?...lean forward a might, sweetie, so I can get yer back. He's older than me anyway, case ya can't tell, a lot older so maybe it's an old person thing. What I've seen of this big bad world I don't feel like turnin' my head either sometimes. But I always do. Cause ya can't not look. What kinda a person would ya be if ya can't at least look? Even with all the bad stuff, pictures they show on the teevee of babies gettin' blowed up and all and floods and shit like that. There. That's all I'm gonna cut, just a titch off the ends is all I did. Now let's get those snarly whiskers of yers under control. Give me yer face and don't move. Pretend yer Jock.

I have no desire to pretend to be the French chef, even for a moment, but given that the girl has scissors to my throat and I can't see a thing for all the soap in my eyes, not moving is reasonable advice.

My, yer a furry thing, ain't ya? I'm just gonna clip a few of these scragglies off so ya look half way decent. I know yer momma wants ya to shave it off but shavin's a pain, if ya ask me. I just do my girl parts and under my arms, and not everyday either, so I can't imagine havin' to do yer face every morning. I'd grow me a beard if I could. And besides, to hell with what yer momma wants. She's some kinda bitch, if ya don't mind me sayin'. The job's hard enough, workin' in people's houses, cleanin' up their messes and bein' nice to them all the time like they're some kinda kings and queens or somethin' . Ain't no reason to treat the help bad, know what I mean? Besides...lift yer chin up there darlin'...besides, maybe they ain't such a big deal after all cause I heard they're havin' some money troubles. Have you heard, hon? Any troubles with money? Why, them Mexicans told Jock they ain't been paid in weeks. What's up with that? She better keep on payin' me and Jock, I'm here to tell ya, or we'll scoot on outta here faster than a pack a dogs on a three legged cat. Ain't gonna be cleanin' no rich bitch's toilet for free, not this gal...open yer mouth, sweetie and I'll get this upper lip, big open, like an O. Like an O hon, you know O? That's it. Now don't move a muscle. There, I'm done with ya. Now let's give ya a good rinsin' off.

The waitress finally moves out of the way and I am able to wash the soap from my eyes. I see her slick white body, not so young herself by all accounts and a few days behind on her own shaving routine. She seems smaller than before, when she's dressed in her starched white uniform, more Argentinean than Appalachian.

I do declare, you could pass for Christ himself, alright.

This is an odd thing to say, I think. Her eyes drop down to my lap and the sorry state of my response to all her attention. Whatever you think is going to happen, sweetie, I would tell her...well, syndromatically, I'm just not up to it.

Hey, maybe ya can't do it, uh? Bein' crippled and all. I didn't think of that to be honest, but I'm kinda turned on right now, you lookin' the way you do. Ya mind if I just sit for awhile?

Which is what she does, her knobby little bottom squished atop my legs and the bone of her white back pressed against my face. I am not used to bearing the weight of others. Perhaps she talks some more while indulging herself on my lap. I can't say. I'm not really here anymore. It's just the waitress and Jesus and a park bench in the rain.

TWENTY-ONE

COSMETOLOGY AND SELF-GRATIFICATION can work wonders on some people. My shower mate, now toweled off and dressed, has reverted back, if back is the proper psychical direction, to her Argentinean self, and is installing me in my never worn shirt and combing through my newly clipped locks. I felt nothing with the waitress on my lap save the discomfort of her slight weight on my tender muscles. And yet, I am aware that something should have been felt, a vestigial sensation I might have once in the forgotten past experienced, probably even enjoyed. These are rare moments that I find myself thinking about who I might have been and not who am I now, and I scour my brain for a relic, some artifact of that long gone era. But nothing. There's nothing to remember. Becoming a fossil is not such a great stretch for the syndromatically afflicted.

The mirror now reports a handsome, casually attired, overly coiffed but hardly divine individual. Nevertheless, the waitress behaves like she's attending to the pope. Amid her servile twittering she let's it slip, *lord*, she calls me. The poor girl, she suffers from her own afflictions. I hope it won't cause her too much distress.

I am uncharacteristically relieved when Lilly arrives. She dispatches the girl to fetch my motor chair.

You look very nice, Gustav, she says, the formal Gustav and not the familiar Gussie, signifying that what is about to happen to me will not be any fun.

She studies my haircut.

I wish she took more off. I told her. Why don't these people ever listen?

Of course they listen, Lilly. Around you that's the only option. The answer is that they don't obey. These people don't like you, have you noticed?

For her efforts at costumery, the woman has de-selected the red uniform in favor of a somewhat chaste and overly precise suit in humble beige.

I'm glad we're taking a little trip together, she continues. *We haven't done this in awhile, have we?*

Lilly pauses a moment, reflexively, waiting for my answer. I say nothing.

Have we, Gustav?

Nothing.

Gussie?...Honey? Are you okay?

We look at one another. Nothing comes out of my mouth. Sweet nothing.

TWENTY-TWO

LILLY'S CAR happens to be English, a fact pointedly expressed to me numerous times by the mechanic, a fervent Anglophobe. Unlike Otto's Italian sports cars, it is spacious and accommodating, the seats are plush but not pillowy and visibility is excellent, an important feature to someone like myself who equates automobiles with rolling coffins. I prefer the backseat with the windows down.

My chair firmly attached to its rack on the rear bumper, we head down the mountain road. Our destination remains the only piece of unrealized bad news, which Lilly presently supplies.

We are going to visit the Hardleys, she informs me. The woman Hardley is the woman Lilly does not like. *You met her before, at a party.*

Lilly has no idea that I don't remember a couple of days ago much less the introductions made in another era. Hers is a prodigious memory. She remembers everything that is important to her in her world: the names of things one buys or is about to buy; who said what to whom about whom and what they were wearing when they said it; whatever she told Otto to do that he has failed to do since the day they met. These are the specifics of her cerebral scrapbook.

I want you to be nice, Gustav, on your best behavior. Will you promise me?

I say nothing.

Gustav? What's happening? I just want things to be better. You know that, don't you?

She's fishing for a yes or a no, but I say nothing.

You won't talk anymore? Gustav? Honey?

Something has happened. Was it the one-sided sex or the clipping of my locks? Nothing is more unsettling than change in progress, and surely I am changing. The awful hiccup that was my speech is gone, and for this I am most pleased. But I have to wonder, am I changing for the better or is this the beginning of the end?

TWENTY-THREE

Whoosh, down the mountain into the valley and through the little town with its frenetic stores, the mad grocery swarming with anxious shoppers all coffeed up and on the prowl for a parking spot closest to the door, closest to the next air-conditioned place. We pass the woman's favorite restaurant, but the patio is abandoned. The heat is too terrible and the blue umbrellas remain undeployed. We turn down a narrowing lane introduced by signage and yellow flowers, and on either side of the street greenish swaths of golf are attended to by furious sprinklers while men in bright shirts and brighter pants drive their buggies like getaway cars.

Around the bend we go and suddenly the road widens to boulevardic proportions. The sky seems bluer here, the grass greener, and everywhere fancy houses are alit upon their gentle inclines like self-satisfying demigods. We have arrived at a world executed exclusively from the pages of a magazine, a drive-thru cavalcade of the unfettered expression of specialness, with one house fancier than the next until it is impossible to be more fancy, just more insistent. Mausoleums for the not yet dead, though traces of the castle motif are still in evidence; the urge to nobility is too great a force here. Moats and drawbridges are implied at every entrance. Heroic statues of snarling lions and agitated horses like pieces to an immense board game keep watch against the lurking hordes. And to each, a fountain, at least one and grand; spitting fish and the overflowing clamshell reign supreme.

Lilly is quiet now, stunned silent by silent Gustav. She relies on me to answer yes and no to her graceless leading questions for the make-believe conversations she contrives for us. My responses, however involuntary, offer her a glimmer of hope that I might someday get better. I would tell her never mind, I am better.

A final whoosh of the car's pompous engine and we are at the gate of the Hardleys.

The Hardley house, the home of the woman she does not like, is not like the other houses in fancyland, and it is most unlike the house on the side of the mountain. It is not built of stones or brick or any other material borne of the earth. There are no angry animals braying on the front lawn, no ludicrous hedges trimmed in puffs and peaks, no fatuous intimations of peerage or the Parthenon. This is a house of glass and geometry, dispossessed of the superfluous, the embellished, devoid of even the most innocuous add-on, more machine than house, an engine of logic over desire and as irrefutable as a fossil. When the iron gates swing open, Lilly steers us timidly up the long black drive and underneath the winged steel canopy that shades the front door. No sooner does the car come to a stop than an older Asian man dressed as a waiter appears beside us, opening Lilly's door and removing my chair from its dorsal mooring. After some clumsy assistance, the chair and I are one.

We linger for an interval in front of two incomprehensibly vertical metal and glass doors that suggest giraffes live here or a family of acrobats that go about perched upon one another's shoulders. At a certain moment, as if cued by an invisible hand, the doors open wide and we are met with a blast of refrigerated air followed by the figure of a tiny, skeletal old woman draped in a sheet of diaphanous white cloth and back lit by a blinding light from a bank of colossal and in all likelihood impossible to clean windows. A hazy mountain of pinkish hair overwhelms her features and it is only a daub of red lipstick that orients her in space.

Darling, pipes the woman, extending her hands to Lilly without moving from the door's threshold.

Obliged, and not happy about it, Lilly approaches the woman and they hug. From my point of view it appears Lilly is embracing a wad of kleenex.

Lilly says, *How nice to see you again...*and at that very moment when I am about to learn the Hardley woman's first name, the waiter emits a sharp bark-like cough (a heavy smoker in all likelihood) and all I can make out sounds very much like...*Ample.* The woman's name is Ample Hardley, to the best of my knowledge.

It is my turn now. In deference to my condition, Ample takes a single step towards me. The remainder of the distance between us appears to be my responsibility.

Gustav dear, come. Let me take a look at you. Her thin, willowy voice dissipates in the air like smoke. She beckons me with a flutter of her bony hands and I activate the chair and close the portion of space between us. *My, how handsome,* she says. Must be the shirt.

With Ample on point we enter the house. It is an enormous, bare space that greets the visitor, the floor is marble and the ceiling is beyond visual confirmation. The general color scheme is decidedly like white but not white or any other color known to mankind. And whatever color glass is. Twin staircases of a transparent hue flank a predominantly invisible elevator shaft, that up down architectural trio I am familiar with in a more garish concoction, and I wonder if the central planning office at fancy doesn't insist on this redundant arrangement in all its units. What I don't see are embellishments of any kind, no squiggles or scrolls, no knick knacks, curios, novelties or the other manifold expressions of dubious whimsy. It is a vacuum of reflections and echoes that says welcome, you have arrived at nowhere and it is grand, and we, your hosts, are too exceptional to accessorize. I imagine these are Lilly's thoughts as Ample leads us onward.

We pass through what Ample calls the living room, an enclosure of mathematically immeasurable proportions that contains but a pair of black leather benches in front of an emotionally distant fireplace. In the corner there's a piano, the size of a car. On the wall behind the piano hangs a series of larger than life paintings depicting variations on a theme; a boy on the ground who may or may not have fallen off his bicycle but he seems to be okay because he's eating a sandwich.

Moving on, the dining room, which is occupied solely by a felled tree surrounded by tree stumps in mourning. I don't believe Lilly is much impressed by the stark expression of Ample's decorative vision, although she says otherwise in a string of runny compliments—not that Lilly is ever at a loss for a string of anything—and it occurs to me that this is probably not the first time she has been to this house. It may not be the first I have been here either. When we come to the kitchen I sense we have arrived at our destination and I am relieved we have been spared a more thorough tour.

Let's have a little snack, shall we? warbles Ample. The waiter, unseen and unheard since our meeting at the driveway, whisks past us in a heated soughing and begins the preparation of a meal. *Come now, let's sit,* the old lady says.

The kitchen table, in size and scope, belies all that I have witnessed thus far. It is a modest, circular affair, topped by a simple white tablecloth with four nondescript chairs about its edge and is crammed into an alcove too small for even this tiny ensemble. The claustrophobics are softened only by a sliding glass door behind the table which provides a view of yet another simple table and chair setup on the patio immediately beyond. Lilly is given the chair on the side with the glass door, the hardest one to get to, while Ample takes the wing and I am placed directly across from Lilly. The fourth chair remains, like a question mark, unoccupied.

Upon a plastic mat of butterflies and flowers, I inspect the dizzy array of forks, knives and spoons laid out in their mysterious logic. A pert white napkin folded in the shape of either a butterfly or a flower awaits my lap. There is something else. Flashing a wan smile at Ample, Lilly pulls my water glass discreetly out of the reach of my graceful arm while shooting me a familiar glance that simultaneously pleads and threatens.

The question posed by the empty chair is soon answered when Ample announces, *I've asked our son to join us. Isn't that marvelous?* I suppose that serves as both an answer and another question, one we will be able to answer now for ourselves, for at that moment Marvelous enters the room.

Marvelous is a large, bald man in pink shorts, a green short sleeve shirt, white socks and black shiny shoes. I am taken aback momentarily by his resemblance to Otto; the hulking stature, the glossy skull, the vaguely proto-sapiens gait, although Marvelous comes off as a much healthier looking specimen, suntanned and trim. And from that I would guess that Otto is the elder of the two, but I could be mistaken. I wonder by what name shall we know this giant Hardley--Leviathan? Hercules? Goliath? If a name has any meaning at all, his must bespeak the substantiality of his mighty frame. So, in the exchange of greetings between son and mother, son and Lilly, and the perfunctory nod from son to son, I am somewhat perplexed to learn that this jumbo has been given the name Young Lamb. Well, he may as well be Button or Twinkletoes. If I were suddenly struck with the power of speech I would not allow myself to utter the name lest I implode with laughter, and even through the stoic lock of my condition I can feel a grin wrinkling across my face. That he should be Young anything is silly enough, but Lamb? Who but a sheep would choose such a thing? My mind is stuck on this wild incongruity as Young Lamb takes the empty seat to my right and instantly shrinks the table to the size of a single teevee tray. I find myself nostalgic for the wide open spaces of the enormous glasstop table.

The pair of Hardleys seem uncomfortable in my syndromatic presence. The old lady demonstrates her cheerfulness.

Tell me, Gustav, how are you doing? How is he doing, Lilly dear?

But Lilly can't bring herself to answer this simple question. She quickly goes all moist on us, and Ample is obliged to comfort her with little pats on the hand and a couple of *there theres.*

The last time I saw him he was talking some. Do you remember the last time we talked, Gustav? she asks me directly.

Gloriously I don't, nor do I say.

He was walking a little too. I see that...

Lilly jumps in. *He was just yesterday. Some days are better than others. Gustav just had a birthday.*

How splendid! Ample chirps.

Happy birthday there, Gus, Young Lamb adds, the breathy boom of his voice are like footsteps on the moon.

We should do a little something...Lin Wee, do we have a little something? Behind me the Asian waiter takes the order. *Good, good. We'll do a little something,* the old lady says to Lilly, patting her on her hands some more. Lilly puts her hands in her lap. Then she says, *Otto gave Gustav a dog.*

This sends Ample into spasms of glee. *A dog! How marvelous! Oh, I love dogs. I just love them. Where's my Precious? Lin Wee, find Precious for me, will you please. You just have to meet Precious, my little man. A dog! I think that's perfectly marvelous. What kind is it?*

Lilly doesn't know because she can't pronouce it. *A big black dog. Very furry.*

Yes, dog fur can be a problem, can't it? the old lady suggests.

I won't let Gustav bring it in the house. I'm so allergic.

Of course, dear. Those pesky allergies. Worse than having a cold, isn't it? *Lin Wee, did you find Precious yet?* The old lady is in fact a little on the unlikable side. She just told Lilly she should be glad that all she has to deal with is her runny nose. She could be the one in the wheelchair, mute and cut off from the world. Lilly's face says she got the message. Which reminds me, I scan Ample's nose for signs of the australopithecine. About the eyes, perhaps, but the nose is inconclusive and my inspection is making her uncomfortable. She throws me that feeble smile she's been using and brings her hand to her face. *Lin Wee?* she calls out again and in comes the Asian waiter with a small dog in his arms.

There's my Precious, the lady gurgles, arms outstretched to take possession of the dog. The little dog seems less than enthusiastic about the transfer and clings to the waiter, but to no avail. Passed onto Ample's lap, it begins to shiver. I sense in it the strongest desire to flee. But Ample hangs on with a practiced grip that defies escape and the dog resigns itself to a thorough mauling. *You'll just love having a dog,* she tells me.

I begin to think about Dog. I wonder if he's all right there with Otto in rhyming mode and the waitress in whatever mode she might be in at the moment. It's a weird world for sure, grueling in its weirdness, and all the more for the unaware, the uninformed, the simple creature that asks only for a regular meal and a quiet place to sleep.

As the Asian waiter busies himself preparing the snack, the two women persist in their efforts to converse. I learn that Young Lamb is just back from a game of golf. There's a husband about somewhere and his name is Lamb Senior. He will not be joining us, thankfully. And there's a great deal of talk about the party they are planning, the whole point of this visit, apparently. The women are very animated on the subject. They can barely get the words out fast enough as the rush of ideas is upon them. Simultaneously, the waiter begins to serve. I pay attention to him, not them. His task seems impossible to perform. Although Ample is easily accessible to her right, the waiter is obliged by a rule I do not understand to present her plate from her left, and to do this he must squeeze by Lilly whose chair leaves little room between it and the sliding glass door. Lilly must understand this rule too and pushes herself closer to the table as the waiter shimmies his way past, his fly brushing against the back of her head. No one except me notices this, the women are lost in their party talk and Young Lamb is lost no doubt in thought of his recent golfage. The waiter deposits Ample's plate on her butterfly mat, an insignificant triangular sandwich, a cookie and a sprig of green for which Ample deigns a satisfied nod. He returns from whence he came, giving Lilly another poke with his pants. I catch his eye. I can tell he thinks it's funny. He would laugh if he could. Instead he delivers another plate, still under the arcane rules of table service, one to Lilly, one to the Young Lamb. No further poking is required. The party talk continues with nary a missed preposition. Finally, the waiter attempts to serve me. Lilly waves him off. *Nothing for him, thank you.*

No snack for you, Gustav? No snack for him, dear? asked our concerned hostess.

He ate, Lilly tells her.

Maybe just a cookie? A birthday cookie. Lin Wee, bring us a cookie.

Lin Wee is quick with the cookie, almost quicker than Lilly. As the cookie plate is being lowered onto my butterflies, I feel my graceful arm cocking as I shall surely send this one deep, but horrified Lilly reaches across the table in time to snatch the plate from the waiter, and all I get is the silverware.

Oh, dear, says the old lady.

I'm so.. says apologetic Lilly

Hmm, says Young Lamb, having dusted off his sandwich in three swift bites, leaving the sprig of green to embellish his empty plate.

TWENTY-FOUR

After the incident at the table I am spared any more of their attention including birthday attention. The two women prattle on about their impending fete in a flurry of interrupted phrases and self-congratulations, with every utterance an affirmation that it will be a party to end all parties. Young Lamb and I are left to stare at the salt and pepper shakers. The women finally take notice of our shared disinterest. It is Lilly, not Ample, that suggests to Young Lamb that he take me on a tour of the house. Odd, I think, as I back my chair away from the table. Why is she the one doing the suggesting? Young Lamb leads on and the clacking at the table soon fades in the distance.

We pass through caverns of glass and steel, abundantly empty places where sunlight and air meet to contemplate one another. Young Lamb is a taciturn guide, thankfully. His singular comment for each new room is *This is where they...*In one room, *this is where they grow unholy.* In another, *this is where they seek the universe.* A room with only a large black ball on the floor is *where they dow sing.* I do not know what dow is, and Young Lamb offers no explanation. He seems as bored with it all as I am.

Not that an explanation wouldn't be helpful. This house is very much not Otto and Lilly's castle on the mountain. I'm not sure what to make of all that I am seeing, or not seeing. There are no cushy couches, no gilded hutches, no bric-a-brac antiquities—there's hardly a place to sit. If I didn't know better I would say the place has been abandoned, the inhabitants have fled and taken all their stuff, although there's probably a girl that still comes twice a week to dust. Why, there's not even a teevee in sight. No hum of the incessant blather is heard around the corner or down the corridor. Otto and Lilly would shut down like deactivated robots here. They require the teevee's harangue and pandemonium to provide them with suitable modes of behavior. This silent place would unravel them.

There are more rooms, more empty silent rooms where they do this or that or the other. I freely admit, these quiet places are a welcome change from the commotion of the mountain. I should be enjoying this, but something's wrong. I sense that everything I've been shown so far is just a show of some kind, a display for the visiting public. In this house of glass and steel, where do they live? Is not a house a home, after all? Where the shoes go. Where the butter is kept. Do these austere Hardleys not slog about in their slippers in the morning looking for a cup of coffee and a teevee show? Are there not desperate ceremonies before a mirror of secret self-loathing? Do they not fart in the hallway or complain about their imagined maladies or bicker and pick at one another over abstract dissatisfactions or a poorly chosen phrase? And at night beneath perfectly realized sheets, do they not copulate like oafish sea mammals seeking redress for the loss of love or what they perceive to be love, which is recast in their fitful dreams as a boat sailing from the shore without them?

I would be gratified to learn soon enough if a bathroom is still a bathroom.

Young Lamb is incurious about my reaction to the tour, and we proceed without commentary up the glass elevator to the second floor. Immediately I detect a change in the overall picture. We traverse a long hallway with solid, regular walls and ordinary doors. We stop at one such door. *This is where she sleeps,* says Young Lamb. *You got to get a load of this.*

He opens the door to a dark room.

We have to go inside so I can shut the door.
I am reluctant to do this.
Come on, then. You'll get the full effect when I close the door.
I nudge the chair forward and Young Lamb closes the door behind us. We are in total blackness.

Okay, here goes. He flicks the light switch and I am enveloped in a bath of absolute pink, pinker than I could ever imagine a color to be. I strain to identify an angle, a surface, the edge of some object one might expect to see in an old lady's bedroom, but all I can make out is a dimensionless veil of electric pink plasma emanating from the ceiling or the wall or who knows where. Instantly my senses go on overload and warning lights begin to flash in the hallways of my cerebral cortex.

Cool, huh? I hear the man say. No, I would tell him. It is the opposite of cool. I must flee, but to where? I jam my chair into drive and run into what seems to be a bed, big and fancy, tented in amorphous clouds of pink. I back up and smack into what might be a table or a dresser. I can only guess. My head is spinning and I realize that my chair is also spinning, round and round. I must leave right now. I strain for a bearing and soon my eyes begin to adjust. I finally make out a real object. It is a teevee. Right there in the middle of the room, as big as a car. So that's how it is. How different this all is from the placid nothingness of downstairs. I fear that if I don't get out of here now that I shall lose control. Maybe Young Lamb senses my panic. The door opens and sunlight pours into this pink horror. I do not remain to take stock of what is now visible. At full throttle I bolt from the room and do not stop.

TWENTY-FIVE

HALF-BLINDED BY THE smoldering singe of the old lady's pink bedroom, I set off down a long corridor in search of the room called this is where they leave the house. The hulky golfer is nowhere in sight.

The carpet is as thick as a mud bog and my chair groans desperately in its forward charge. Where am I? This doesn't even look like the same house. The walls are made of wall and the doors are made of door. I consider turning back in hopes of regaining the trail, but then I come across one particular wall that is covered with all sorts of neatly framed photographs.

What do we have here? Rubbing my eyes hard I find some focus. Why, it's the Hardley family gallery. Yes, there's Ample and Young Lamb, caught in an alternate concoction of timespace; she's just as scary and he has hair. Here they are again, joined by a short, thin fellow with an enormous head; papa, perhaps. There's always a papa. He's sporting one of those floppy-lipped fish smiles and looking pretty pleased with himself. And another, the three of them, the old lady seated, her massive hair restated in yellow, her two men standing beside her like sedated sentries. Here's papa shaking hands with a very important person...and papa standing on a stage shaking a book and perhaps yelling something. He seems a bit worked up. A headshot of a less aged Ample, very fancy, her hairdo not entirely contained in the frame, a glint of tear in her eye. Here's a younger Young Lamb, playing the piano and looking quite pained about it. There are several of these, the dramatic musician, younger, older, hairy, hairless...but remarkably unchanged from the ears down. Time has spared him all but the follicles. Some more photos of papa standing around with other big-headed types, shaking hands and flashing their fish smiles...and others, faded, of strangers from another epoch dressed in their gloomy suits and not so smiley. I think about the only photograph I can remember, grandfather Gustav in his oversized army suit, the ancient soldier boy.

Beyond the photo gallery, the corridor starts to widen. Nothing more on the walls, just a fire extinguisher. I press on. The carpet transitions to a smooth grey concrete and the floor begins to slope gradually downward. I feel the chair accelerate slightly and I throttle back to brake. I come to a pair of metal doors, the one side ajar, and with nowhere else to go, I open the door and pilot my chair across the threshold. No sooner am I inside when the door slams shut and my chair and I are hurling wildly down a steep decline, sliding headlong, now backwards, into the darkness. At any moment I shall surely crash.

But I don't crash. Evidently, I'm ramp-proof. The floor levels out, the chair responds to my command and I come to a stop. Now I find myself in an enormous room, like some kind of theater with lights in the rafters and tangles of heavy wire covering the floor. Great pieces of strange equipment block my way. I am at the foot of some sort of stage. Above me, stirring in the shadows, I see a figure on the stage, a man. He approaches. Now the figure is standing right over me, lost in the lights, looming while I squint. I stare at the figure until I can no longer bear the strain on my eyes and am obliged to look away. When I open my eyes again, the man is no longer over me; he is behind me and guiding my chair up onto the stage.

As you can see, we're handicapped enabled around here. In fact, it's a specialty; the sick, the lame, the existentially lazy...they flock here like baffled sheep. Well, not here, but you'll see.

The man gestures to a dimly lit booth in the far corner where a bald man waves back.

Are we ready to go, the man says to no one in particular. A boomy voice answers from what seems like everywhere, *All set, Dad.*

The man says to me, *Gus, I'm going to turn you around here like this and put you right here on this little white ecks on the floor like this....Lamb, how does that look to you?*

Lamb replies, *Perfect. Keep him right there. I'm turning on the green screen now.*

There's a flash and I turn my head to see that the wall behind us has turned a hideous electric green.

The man says, *You don't want to stare at the green monster for too long. She'll eat you up. I want you to look straight ahead, out there into the darkness. Good lad. Okay, son, let's have the big teevee.*

Out of the black void flickers a monster of a teevee screen, the largest I am sure I have ever seen, perhaps the largest in existence. And what are we watching? I see a stage—no, this stage. The one the man and I are currently occupying, with the green wall behind us. I am on teevee.

The man calls out into the darkness, *Now give me my Sunday best; the big chair, all by itself, and all the usual geegaws, the bedizziments and magical festooneries, and let's have some flowers, lots of flowers...hmm, what do you say, white roses is honor of our estimable friend here, Prince Gustav.*

Nice touch, Dad, responds Young Lamb. There's another flash and the stage is transformed—not the one I'm on but the one on the screen, which I'm also on. This is very confusing. Somewhere, somehow, something, the screen I suppose, has become the fanciest thing imaginable. The big chair is an edifice of goldishness and shimmering spanglies that is only incidentally a chair, and on either side a pair of crystal chandeliers hang from nowhere like clusters of iridescent fruit. Behind all this a twisting staircase, more twinkling goldy gilded shiny sparkles, winds upward to no particular place, to the clouds. And everywhere, vases of unabashed white roses.

Ah, that's lovely. Our little tabernacle, you gotta love it. Okay, Lamb. Put me in the chair.

The big screen flickers and there's the man sitting on the fancy throne... right here, or there. My head snaps back and forth from the green miasma to the images appearing on the big teevee.

Helluva thing, isn't it? I call it the reality machine. It's got a technical name, several I suppose, but for the life of me I can't remember that stuff. But Young Lamb there is a wizard, he is. Watch this. Okay, Maestro, bring on the faithful. Let's have ourselves a party.

Flash and flash, and there are people everywhere, an absolute multitude of them, packed solidly inside some imaginary coliseum as far as the eye can see. Some are seated, their gazes transfixed to a point that feels uncomfortably like it might be me. Others are standing with the hands clasped together and their eyes full of moisture, trembling slightly. However, the great majority are lost in the shadows, far, far away. But their sheer volume is inescapable and beyond comprehension.

*Look at them, my blubbering darlings! Got to have themselves a good cry on their Sunday mornings. Get **it** out of there systems, that nasty niggling **it**. Know what I mean? Every get that thing, that **it**?*

I couldn't say.

Lambent Hardley's the name. A great pleasure it is to make your acquaintance. The man extends his hand. My graceful arm swings around syndromatically and we shake.

They call you what...not Gustav? Gustav sound likes a goddamn Prussian cavalry officer, which clearly you are not. Or perhaps just Gus? Gus is a great name for a tough guy, honest as an oak. I like Gus. But you're not Gus either, are you? You don't look very tough and I don't think you're being very honest with us or your mama.

Lambent paces a slow circle around me while sizing up my character flaws, but on the screen he is seated on the throne all smug and big-headed.

One hears about the famous Gustav Deal. The wives talk, you know. There's a form of gossip based entirely on the phrase, Isn't it a shame.... You and your mama are popular topics. But you probably know all about that, don't you? Because they talk right in front of you, because they think you have squash for brains and can't understand a word. Why I'll bet they don't even bother to spell things out like they would for a child. You're not even that to them, are you? You're more like a dog, a furry, somewhat sickly and not altogether well-groomed dog. And I'm sure you know all about that too.

Right now I know nothing about anything.

Say, Young Lamb apologies for leaving you off like that, but I needed him here in the studio on a technical matter. Helluva engineer, that boy of mine. Every week he puts on a show all by himself from that booth up there, all those buttons and switches, I get lost in the complexities. But Lamb's an absolute magician. All I have to do is stand here and talk. Any idiot can do that. It's his magic that fills this studio with the simpering faithful, thousands of them, millions if he wanted to...turn this place into the goddamn Vatican at Easter, he could. But people wouldn't buy that. You got to give them what they can wrap their heads around. You want them awestruck, not dumbstruck.

I decide to leave. I give my chair the gas but I'm stuck, the wheels are caught on some cables.

Damn cables, I know. That's the other thing I have to do. Not trip. It's harder than you think. But you don't see those wires and such on the screen. Lamb takes them right out. Puts down a shiny marble floor right under my feet. Love to get rid of the cables though.

No can do, Dad, says the bassooned voice of Young Lamb.

Say, I've got an idea. Lambent, let's put our young friend here in today's audience..right up front.

That we can do, says the younger Lambent.

Another flash, and there I am on the enormous teevee screen sitting in the front row of the stadium packed with non-existent people.

Oh, that's good. That's very good. What do you think, Gus? Ever been on teevee before? Exciting, isn't it? Care to multiply the experience? Lamb?

Flash, flash, and the person next to me turns into me, and the next one too, and the next until all the people on the screen are copies of me.

Unaccustomed as I am to remembering people, I suddenly

recognize Lambent Hardley. He is the man who was screaming about Jesus on the teevee while the waitress cleaned Lilly's toilet.

Bravo, maestro! Gustavs everywhere. Love It! Love it! Now, let's have a few of you on stage too. Maestro?

Blink, and a queue of wheelchairs appears on the stage, with me in them, rolling up to either side of Lambent's big chair.

There you are, my boy. Infinitely realized in the electronic realm.

Sure enough, I am everywhere, at least on the big screen. Legions, oceans of me in my birthday shirt. My mind is swimming. I try to back my chair out of its rut, but to no avail.

Hey, stick around. You'll want to see this. Son, give me the lights and give me the noise.

And once again the screen is transformed: the golden staircase, the fancy throne, the white roses, the vast, immeasurable throng of me, everything illuminated by the sweep of white hot searchlights to and fro, and Lambent, who is either seated or standing right next to me, or what appears to be me, takes a step toward the edge of the stage and the other Lambent, the electric Lambent rises from the chair to join himself. All manner of hollering and moaning and crying out fills the room, impossible lamentations emanating from the mouths of countless Gustavs. The vibrations of this cacophony travel through the wheels of my chair and into my brain.

That's what it is, says the senior Lambent. *Welcome to teevee land, young Gustav. The electric dream from which we never awake. Shall we begin? C'mon then. Stand forth. Isn't that what they say, stand forth?*

Now the two Lambents are one. He begins to speak into the void.

We have with us this blessed day on the stage of our humble tabernacle, right here, right now, a young man but perhaps not so young but so thoroughly afflicted, so gravely damaged, and he comes to us today seeking the benefaction of the cosmic commander that he may one day walk and talk and stand tall among us imbued with the spirit of the almighty one. Behold our pilgrim, whose name is known as Gustav, an empty, pitiful vessel bereft of the holy spirit. Today he asks for the lord's forgiveness, not in words but simply by his presence among us. O lord, he calls out to you from the heart, from the depth of his imprisoned soul, from the sublime interior of his disconnected totality that he might feel thy healing touch and be restored. Let us rejoice and praise him.

On the giant teevee the throng of Gustavs bow their heads and echo Lambent's words, *Praise him.*

Amen. Let us pray. Dearest great one, holiest of holies, master of the universe, shedder of light, grantor of gravity, he who sees every last little thing that tumbleth from the treetops...witness the tears we shed today for our brother, a piteous mess of a man, a waste of good protoplasm, lost and alone, wandering the desert like a broken nomad, and the power of your blithe spirit absent from his heart. Whither thou goest, brother Gustav, upon your electric chariot? The night seems bleak and cruel, and the corridors of your lamentable journey are strewn with the corpses of forsaken angels. Dear brother, how do you abide the loneliness, rent from the bosom of mankind and our lord's tender mercy? How deep is the chasm of your soul that the words you long to utter cannot locate the membranes of natural articulation? How high is the pinnacle you wish to scale that your legs are unwilling to take that bold first leap antrorse? O brother, you have not been forsaken. It is you who have forsaken the lord. Let us praise him.

All the Gustavs cry out, *Praise him.*

Yes, praise him. Our lord and master of the heavens, whose graceful hand is into everything and whose ears pick up even the wretched mute's lamentations to thee, hear our prayer! Let this miserable slave rise and cast off these cursed chains, command that he stand forth and utter a coherent phrase or two to thy glory. We pray that he beseech from thee on this day a monad of salvation by your divine grace, foreswear this pretense of affliction and once and for all, cut it out!

All the Gustavs repeat, *Cut it out.*

There is a name for this affliction, too terrible to pronounce for it is the evil one's locution. Syn, from the Greek meaning the fundamental decency lacking in man for which we must constantly apologize. And Drome, meaning, well, it means a few things actually; a combining form meaning running or course, then there's the region in France, also a river, and there's an airport reference...

(a voice from the darkness) *Dad, if you could remember what we're trying to do here...*

Thanks, son. You're right, I'm wandering. Let's pick it up at the drome bit.

Drome, drome, drome...also from the Greek, signifying a great edifice, an arena where man's defects contest for supremacy. Syndrome, O cursed demon of the mind. Only the evil one could conjure a word more foul and odious. Banish this word from our lips, father, that the thing itself would cease to exist. Or sayeth otherwise, something like great big houses have great big problems, for this we can handle. And what is a house but the heart. And what is the heart but an organ of the body, and the body but an organ of the cosmic one. So what then is so special about the heart that it would deign to control the ben-e and mal-e of our factions? What manner of organ is this sayeth this troubled man who has come to the lord, that I am struck mute and crippled by the beating of a muscle and the pumping of my blood? And the lord will sayeth unto the man, I shall tear down this demon from thy breast, and peal away from thine eyes this mask of turmoil that thee may see my glory, for I am the one, the only, the lord almighty, father in heaven, creator of the cosmos, the light of all life, big man in the sky, the holy ha cha cha!

Dad...

Sorry, Lamb. You know that last one's my favorite.

I'm bringing the lights down. Maybe that'll help.

Sure. Let's keep rolling. Give me a shout out.

The Gustavs cry, Amen.

Brother Gustav, I say unto you, let your yes be yes and your no be no. But remember this for true: a windowless soul is but a wall, and the seeds of wisdom sprout weeds in the desert of the thirsty man's mind. A glass is only as full as the water is wet. The board is straight, the earth is round, but everywhere houses. No thing has its own name save the one thing which has no name. So be gone! this fanciful affliction, this damnable disorder of the mind. Enough of your caviling, your remonstrations, your nasty moods. O heart! Buck up a little, why can't you? For the moment or two you share the planet, why make it so hard on others? Do not others have their troubles? Are not others entitled to their brief interludes without the fulsome beating of your anxious drum? A terrible personality disorder is not a life sentence, brother Gustav. It is the common curse from which all men suffer now and then, when love's glorious beacon appears to be shining insufficiently upon them. Yes, too little love and too much are monstrous; only the right amount will do. This is our complaint, but it needn't be. You be the mighty creator. You alone have the power to cast off these weary proclivities. As the absence of light is dark, so is the absence of dark light. One candle is worth a thousand priests. Banish them, brother! Release your blackbirds, be free of them! Verily I say unto you, the mind is a heathen mad for its own demise! Uncouple yourself from this bleak humanity and rise, rise above this mortal station, this self-imposed decrepitude, this so unnecessary disorder of the spirit. Rise like the sun on the first morning in paradise and bask in the holy warmth of decent, righteous, proud, glorious...normalcy!*

Amen, cry the Gustavs. *Amen*

Halleluiah, cries out Lambent

Halleluiah, they, we repeat again and again.

Praise him! Praise him! screams Lambent over the tumult.

Halleluiah... Praise, Praise the lord! chants the crowd of me.

Lambent falls silent. Never have I enjoyed teevee less. On the big screen the multitude of iterations of me are bawling like babies, their arms, graceful and otherwise waving hysterically, grasping at some unknown thing. Voices that never could be mine are crying out, wailing, moaning, a piteous yowl, pained and ecstatic, sobbing, blubbering Gustavs, frenzied, delirious Gustavs, Gustavs possessed by some improbable affliction or the electric ether. Gustav the madman. Gustav the raving lunatic.

The camera's eye moves across the ocean of myself, the immensity of my numbers shimmering like heat coming off the desert when taking in the view.

Of course, I know what's going on here. Lilly. I would tell her that this attempted cure is worse than any affliction, as is often the case when the diagnosis is made by the afflicted, and Lambent as Lilly's proxy in the matter, suffers mightily, syndromatically from a disease with which I am not familiar, a malady with no name that has infected the lot of them. And now, having passed through yet another gauntlet of salutary scrubbing, I am the worse for it, exhausted and spent, and I would not describe the effort as well-intentioned or, that other overused word, loving, for surely this is the opposite of love which is more famous than the truth and equally misapplied; in fact, I would say that love and truth together conspire to afflict more misery than any two artifices devised by the creature sapiens sapiens. The words, that is, not the things themselves. The name of a thing is always a lie.

The lights come up and all the screens go dark. I am transported by an unseen porter off the stage of Lambent Hardley's electric tabernacle and through the labyrinth of glass and steel. The urge to sleep is greater than I can bear. The trip seems interminable but at last I am brought to a stop in a place that is vaguely familiar. There on the wall is the boy with the sandwich and beside me is the enormous black piano. Young Lamb is seated at the keys. The others, Lilly, Lambent Senior, Ample and the little dog have taken seats by the fireplace. The hammers in my head are nearly beating me unconscious and I close my eyes to try to bring myself some comfort, but it is not to be. A thin, willowy voice announces that her son will now play for us a piece of his own devising. The briefest of silences ensues followed by the loudest of rackets. Young Lamb lunges into the instrument, pounding out chunks of sound with such uncontained ferocity that I immediately feel myself imperiled by the threat of sonic shrapnel. The urge to cover my face is exceeded only by the need to cover my ears, but my hands will not move. I am paralyzed by the kinetic chaos of the giant pianist's own significant paws which are furiously slamming away at the piano as though it were stone he's banging on, as though his very survival depended on it. The clang and clangor, like so many shards of glass and steel being run over by a lawnmower now threaten to induce in me that dreaded tremor. I feel my graceful arm vibrating in unison with the terrible tumult that floods the room, the house, the universe. I struggle to hold on like a sailor cast overboard, grasping for a lifeline. I gulp for a single breath but the air in the room has been displaced by the torrent of notes emanating from the maw of the black box. Lilly and the others are sitting placidly with their ridiculous smiles unaware of my impending disaster. Only the little dog seems affected by this musical assault. Detaching itself from Ample's lap, it scurries from the room. Oh, if only I could myself, but my arm is quivering out of control, and it now seems inevitable that at any moment I shall lapse into that most terrible state. When I think I can hold off no longer, Young Lamb lets go a fusillade of sound that requires all his fingers and both forearms to produce. I close my eyes and feel myself tipping over the abyss, but just then the music stops. I draw a breath and step back from the edge. The others clap their polite claps and Young Lamb, covered in perspiration, nods a nod. Mama Hardley squeaks a couple of bravos and the giant turns to me and whispers, *Feeling better?*

For a moment I feel nothing. No pain, no anguish, no terror. I sense only the rapid beating of my heart. But then, it is a familiar warmth that passes over and through me. Young Lamb exclaims, *Gosh, old man, you've pissed yourself.* Lilly rushes over just as the hot trickling of amber liquid reaches the snow white rug. And how quickly she dissolves into a paroxysm of tears and grief. Ample is right there to comfort her, *Don't you worry now, dear...*and Lambent too, *It's perfectly natural...*but the woman is not consoled. *Dear God, help me, help me please God,* she cries, *I dropped my baby...I dropped him...I dropped him....*

The four of them are standing over me and my conspicuous urine. Lilly is wailing and moaning like a woman possessed. Right away the Asian waiter is here with a big white towel to mop me up. Lilly gets on her knees and with the end of the towel furiously dabs at the puddle on the rug. She looks up at me with her ugly, gooey tears, desperate, defeated, uncorked eons of turmoil rolling down her makeup stained cheeks, and in her own wordless way she pleads with me...please, please, PLEASE be somebody else.

I cannot be, I would tell her. I would not be.

In the meantime the Hardleys three have disappeared. When

Lilly sufficiently recovers herself, the Asian waiter escorts us to the front door. From here, through the bank of colossal windows behind the stairs, I spot Lambent Senior and Ample in the backyard walking hand and hand and altogether naked beneath a resplendent sun.

TWENTY-SIX

Lying in bed, I can only think about how tired, how utterly exhausted I am. I look forward to forgetting this last bit of therapy. Dog's clumsy weight is pressing up against me, an embrace of sorts, and the gentle rhythm of his breathing carries me into a deep sleep...

...Dark clouds form and a cool wind stirs, rattling the windows and shaking the blue umbrellas. Trees quiver with inappropriate glee at the approaching storm. The woman is standing at the entrance to the hedgerow maze wearing only the sheer four hundred dollar nightie she got at the village boutique. Her legs are exposed, her feet are bare and she's cold and frightened and highly discommodiated by the whole experience. Her nightie billows up in the wind. She tries to hold it down as she is not too keen about flashing even though she's had her hoohoo professionally manicured. I must look like that famous actress in that movie, she thinks. Now she is obliged to enter, of this much she is sure, but her legs are paralyzed with fear. She cries out, *I'm afraid,* and a distant voice replies, *So what else is new?*

Peering deep into the menacing portal of the larybinth, every impulse in her says turn back, run for safety, run back to the house now, to the warm bed waiting for her, to her Egyptian cotton sheets with the thread count off the charts, and of course back to stupid Otto, snoring his rhymes, and that faux manly French soap smell mixed with cigar stink permeating every crevice of the bedroom until she's ready to hurl, and how he farts in bed like an old cow, like a sick old cow that's also lactose intolerant. *I should want to run back to that?* she asks herself out loud and takes her first tentative steps into the maze.

The wind freshens, heavy clouds swirl above the steep thicket of black leaves that shake like menacing ghosts standing sentry duty. Slowly her eyes adjust to the forbidding path before her. Pots of colorless flowers line the way, but which way, she wonders, *If I don't know where I'm going is left still left and right still right?* And what she wouldn't give for a pair of slippers and a warm robe. The desire to go shopping is nearly more than she can bear. *There must be a store around here somewhere,* she utters, and no sooner do the words leave her lips than a row of shops appears among the brambles.

Dress shops and shoe stores and places to buy a handbag. All very lovely, she thinks. Unfortunately, the doorways to the best stores are blocked by a tangle of thorny rose bushes and sharp slivers of broken vases. She presses on, examining the merchandise displayed in the inviting windows and imagining herself in that gown or those shoes until she comes upon one particular store, a rather rundown and not at all quaint place with an open door for her to enter.

She steps inside the dank, musty shop, but there's no one in sight. The place smells of wet cardboard and cabbage soup. Her first thought is to flee, to run away as fast as she can. There is something painfully familiar about all this, something from a distant past she most desperately does not want to remember. But she doesn't leave. *I ought to find something to wear,* she tells herself.

The selection is quiet meager, a few flimsy racks of dresses, not at all her style. And the strangest thing; the more she handles the merchandise the plainer everything becomes, right before her eyes. One dress when she goes to check the label turns into a filthy burlap smock, another actually falls to shreds in her hands. And the shoes...why, if her feet weren't killing her she wouldn't give the sorry selection a second look. These are hardly shoes at all, she thinks, more like slippers of the cheapest sort, fit only for a prison yard. *This is the worst store I've ever seen,* she declares.

From behind a backroom curtain a small, haggard old woman appears and gives her a terrible start, for she recognized her immediately.

Mama! she exclaims.

You're late, the old lady tells her. *Where have you been? Off running around with your fancy friends again, I suppose. I can't run this shop by myself, Lillian. Now help me get ready. We'll be getting busy any moment now.*

I'm lost Mama, she says. *In the bushes. I've been running and running and I have no clothes or shoes and I'm cold and tired and frightened.*

There's never anything good enough for you to wear, is there? the old woman says. *Snivel and kvetch, that's all we ever get from you. Why God should send me such a daughter, I don't know.*

*But, Mama...*the woman falls silent. Looking around the dingy surroundings, the peeling wallpaper, the floor covered with sawdust, she becomes very sad and even more forsaken. *Mama, where's Papa?*

Your father's away. You know, away. Don't you know away? What's happened to you? What have done with my daughter?

Oh, Mama, it's me! It's your Lillian.

My Lillian had such pretty hair, like chestnuts. But you, with this fakatah red, like one of those women. And what have you done to your nose?

I've been searching, Mama, searching. Nothing is right. Nothing is the way it ought to be.

Such drama! Searching, searching, Mama. Nothing is right...so how is anything different with you? You go off with your goy husband and you think everything is going to change, poof, like that. You think everything is perfect because you can buy things in a store? Well, this is a store. Buy something.

The old lady busies herself arranging the slim inventory as the woman watches and waits. And just as her mother predicted, customers begin to come, a long, single file of the most bedraggled human beings the woman has ever seen; shoulders slumped and eyes cast downward, silent, dispirited shoppers who show no interest in even looking at the merchandise. Instead, they begin to swirl around her like they were the water and she was the drain, round and round until she can't move, till she can barely breathe, pushing against her, squeezing, swallowing her up. She strains to cry out, to scream...but what, she thinks. *What should I say?*

Meanwhile, from a vertiginous height, like a soaring eagle, the poet scans the horizon. Below, the intricate weave of the hedgerow maze. Above, a blazing sun scorches a cloudless dome of blue and brown; velvet mountains shimmer in the distance.

Whither hath thou wanderest? intones the poet as he descends the ladder, a carpenter's tool, and sets out to seek his love.

Into the dense complexities of the labyrinth he commences, down corridors promising and lost, left turns that lead right or nowhere, along curious paths only to rediscover a familiar bend. But he will not be deterred.

Further on, the hedge begins to diminish, and soon the towering ramparts are no more than withered sticks, and he is able to step over them and into a clearing of sorts, a flat spot. The sounds of rushing water greet him and he is glad. *Yes, this gentle brook of my own devising beneath a canopy of wholly grown trees. Surely my love is here.*

Where you been? the woman asks curtly. She occupies one of a matched pair of lawn chairs beneath a blue umbrella.

My love, at last I've found you! cries the poet, rushing to her. *How long I have searched.*

Yea, sure. Searching. says the woman. *I've been lost in these fucking bushes for hours, half naked and barefoot. Since when do you have hair?*

My darling, darling Lilly, fairest flower....

*And what's with the get up? Where'd you get that puffy shirt? Did **she** buy that for you?*

Tea cup, angel...whatever do you mean? There is you. Only you.

You look thin. Doesn't she feed you, what's her name, Mona?

Cindy. She is nothing. A mere scribe, an amanuensis who records the words of love I sing to you, my everything.

Horseshit. A-man-you-blah-blah. Don't think I don't know what's going on. Schtupping your secretary. How poetic. How...rhythmic. I'm on to you, Mr. Shakespeare fucks up everything he touches. You think that little chippy is going to stick around after you're broke?

Love! All this wild talk. These fitful imaginings. Let me...

DON"T sit down.

As you wish, my rose petal. Here, I've written a poem. Let me recite it for you, conjured from my heart bursting with devotion for you.

I don't want to hear any more of your stupid poems.

Please, my beacon of light, my fountain of desire.

You're so full of shit.

Whilst upon my quest for thee I devised it. And declaim it for thee I shall.

To sleep, perforce to dream?
Of course, to dream.
Sweet creamy dreams of lust and lilies,
Mounds and mons of marigolds
Twixt thy seedy sighs.
Of loping and hoping and doping
O're this dandelion'd mind of mine,
Dreaming of what the id did.
Where the egos, me goes.
A bite of time and my droll prole soul
Days go bye; but come night I scour
The verdant vacuum, odious, otiose maze,
Labyrinth of longing and memory.
My sullied sail set upon your wistful wind,
From high to nigh my beckoned urge
    did race,
At long last love did these syndromes
of despair erase.

Bullshit.

You never liked my poems.

What's to like? Odio-odio maze? My weedy thighs? My wind? Everything that comes out of your mouth is bullshit.

You weren't even listening.

What do you mean my wind? What about your wind, huh? Your sail ever catch a whiff of your wind? Do you have any idea how ridiculous you are? Do you have even the vaguest idea what I put up with with you? Your growling and groaning at every last little thing that displeases you, the non-stop bellyaching lord of the manor fartbag attitude, the moods, the snap on a dime temper tantrums, your stupid cars you can't even fit into...And what about your son? What about that? Where are you for him who could use a father now and then, but you're too busy with that con game you call a business that's going in the toilet because you're too big a cheat to do something normal, like normal men do. And how am I supposed to live then, Mr. Big Deal, when they cart you off? Mr. Great Big Huge Deal can't get a decent present for his only child on his birthday but he can boink the girl at the office. Asshole. Get off the phone.

I gotta take this call.

Gimme that goddamn phone, you son of a bitch. Get back here....

TWENTY-SEVEN

I wake with my head pounding and the taste of French tuna in my mouth. There seems to be no stepping away from this world, even in sleep. I wonder how along I've been out. Through the bedroom window the desert has given up its light completely. The sermon to repair me is a fading memory, thankfully, but I can't get that music out of my head. Nearly did me in. And Lilly crying in the car on the way back. Over and over she muttered to herself, Jesus Effing Christ. Jesus never shames. Jesus never wets his pants. Not like her own son, the flaw in the birthday shirt.

What's that lump in my bed? I sense a furry mass. Right, I have a dog. Twitching in his sleep, a dreamer like his bedmate. Be sure to dream your own dreams, that's my advice. I stroke his massive head. Okay. We're still okay.

My whole body aches. No charge left in my legs, that's for sure. I don't see my power chair anywhere, just old lefty. It'll have to do. Where are my clothes? Someone's undressed me. I don't like other people undressing me. I am not without some capacity. They should understand that by now. Jesus effing Christ.

My rustling has waked the dog. He comes out of sleep ready to go like he's equipped with his own on/off switch. I'm still groggy and not ready to do much of anything. I'm starving. Maybe there's a snack in a my little fridge. We check it together. The dog is highly interested in the possibilities. But nothing. Not even a sliver of cheese. No one's bothered to stock it. Sorry, Dog. The cupboard is bare. Let's go see what we can find.

I take Dog outside, aware even with my limited capacities that dogs need to go outside. Evidence of his liberal use of the yard is beginning to pile up. Inturdgence: a new word I coin for Otto, but he'll have to come up with it himself. I'm not talking.

All seems quiet at the increment. A soft glow from the stove fire on the upper floor. Little legs dangling from the edge. I think about the air conditioner in the shack. The desert is not so quick to give up its heat.

Dog and I take the back path around the increment, kitchen bound.

Rounding the corner, we both try to be quiet, but the chair has a squeak to it. A figure emerges from the gloom, a big man with a big brimmed hat that covers his face. I feel a twinge of despair. No more tonight, please. A moment's peace, not too much to ask. But it's not a figure, it's Penzio, dressed like a Mexican.

Hey Gustavo, What you know? Come over here, away.

He speaks barely above a whisper. I assume he doesn't want to wake the others. We follow the path to a spot between the ruin and mother seashell and stop beside one of the walk lights. He turns to me.

We make no noise, eh? Tell the dog. What, you no sleep? How come? You no look so good. Maybe you sick, eh?

When I don't reply he gives me a look.

You want I get mama for you?

I give him a single shake of my head. I don't need mama.

Okay. That's good. I no want to get her anyway. I no want to get nobody. I hiding a little. I no tell you why. I live with the meheecanos now. They make a nice bed for me up top.

Besides looking ridiculous in the big hat, Penzio doesn't seem quite himself, either. By now he should be talking up a storm. Instead he fidgets silently while the dog pees against the side of the mountain.

After a while he says, *Too much trouble for me here, Gustavo. Poleetzia. You know what it is, Poleetzia?*

I give him the anti-nod.

Always the cops. They come soon, I think. I tell you, Gustavo, the cook and his wife, they no good. They make too much trouble for Penzio. They say I do the lock but I no do it. You know I no do it. Why I do it? Maybe they do it. The French they are worse than the English. I no trust them. When they come here I say to myself they trouble for sure but what can I do? I tell your mama, watch those two but she no listen. She like his eggs. Now I hide.

Penzio begins to shake his head with grief or despair, there's no telling for sure, his head going one way, his hat the other. He falls silent again. This is all very unusual. I think about my stomach and reach for the wheels of my chair. Then he comes up with something else to say.

I no understand why you are the way you are. I ask your mama and she say one thing. I ask your papa and he say another. I say to myself, poor Gustavo, no can walk, no can talk. All by himself all the time, planting the pots. This is no life for a man. But then I think maybe you are a happy man, because I know about unhappy men. I am my whole life with unhappy men. Some men have no money and they are very unhappy, too much work, too many bambeenos, the way of the world. Other men, they have money, too much money I think and they are unhappy too. Life is a balance for all things. But I say, maybe Gustavo knows something unhappy men do not know. What is this something, I ask? I wish you to tell me this because I am unhappy too, always running, always hiding out. I come to America so I no have to run no more. No more bullshit, I think, in America, but here I find more bullshit than all the other places I live. Here in America you have more of everything. Here in America I get lost. A man like me gets lost in this world, same in one place as in another. And I think sometimes we want too much from this world, more than she can give. The world no cares what we want. Is crazy, eh? To be happy in this life is not enough. A man wants this life and then another life, a forever and ever life with the father in heaven. One happy life and one perfect life. This is what people want to believe, so we get lost. I tell you, Gustavo, to believe, this is easy. Maybe everybody they are lost in the world. I am sad today because I go soon, but there are no more places for me to go. I can believe no more. At last I am lost for good. Maybe I go to the moon, eh? In a rocket ship made with the space metal. What do you think? Poof, to the moon?

Unlikely the mechanic will go to the moon or anywhere else, for that matter. Chances are he's stuck here, like the rest of us.

At that moment I feel a trembling in the earth, a rumbling and a grumbling, a vaguely reminiscent humhumming up the drive. A truck, I think, and a fairly siginificant one by the sound of things. More commotion coming our way.

I turn to Penzio, but he is gone. So I head off, and no sooner do I round the corner and there, coming up the drive, an enormous beast, a dragon of a truck and such an odd serpent too; a driveway atop a driveway atop a truck, nimbly twisting its way around the horsehead fountain. It comes to a stop and lets out a horrific fart, then starts up again, pulling forward and back, over and over in short, urgent turns until its tail in aligned with the top of the ramp to the underground garage. Dog is enormously disturbed by the beast and begins barking for all he's worth. Some rough looking men get out of the truck and head down into the garage. Pretty soon there's more rumbling, very familiar, the glurbling of furrarees. One by one, up the ramp they come, right up onto the truck. First on top and then the bottom until the beast is loaded with all of Otto's furrarees. And for good measure, Otto's and Lilly's cars too. The one I don't see is the one that was thrown in. The men get back into the serpent and off they go, removing the lower portion of the fountain as they pass. The tower of clamshells topples over and smashes all over the driveway.

Well, that was something different. And where's Otto, I wonder? Looking around and about...and then up, there, on the roof, Otto, with his business buddies. They're all on the roof and Otto is jumping up and down and waving his arms and yelling about something, while the others are not so much standing as crouching and clinging. When the noisy truck clears the gate I can make out what he's yelling about. *Go on, then. Go. Take them. I give them to you, you animal fuckers. I don't want them. Hear me? Take them all. I'm okay. I'm just fine. I can take care of myself. Hear me? I'll get more. Lots more. I'll own them all before I'm finished so fuck you. Fucking fuck fucking you. Do you hear me, you bastards? I'll have them all...*

He goes along in that vein for awhile, but I have to leave. I've heard Otto scream before. At least he's stopped rhyming.

TWENTY-EIGHT

THE HOUSE IS QUIET NOW. Dog and I are in the kitchen feasting on cheese and crackers. His appreciation of the meal is breathtaking. Long after I've had my fill the dog asks for more and he's very polite about it, sitting in front of me with his sturdy log legs, taking the cheese from my hand without touching my fingers with his significant teeth. I feed him until the store is spent. Now we are all truly cheeseless.

The sun will be up soon. There's a private place I know about, more private than the shack or the underground garage, and I decide we should go there.

The journey is not an easy one. We have to go around back of the pool house and skirt behind the spot where the pool pump is located, to an opening in the wall. It's a tight fit for the chair and Dog waits for me to show him the way. We take it slow as we are right on the edge of the flat spot where the mountain returns to vertical, the precipice here being unguarded by even the short curb that surrounds the patio, and the path is not laid out with flat stones like the path behind the house. The way is bumpy and jagged. I show the dog how we must stay close to the wall and follow the tracks made by the wheels of my chair from countless previous expeditions. At the end of the path there's a place to stop and watch the sun come up.

Dog proves sure-footed to the task and we obtain our perch without incident. The sky is clear and full of stars. The evening air is cool and refreshing. I surprise Dog with a piece of cheese I pocketed on the sly. He dispatches it in a single gulp. I take a long breath and exhale slowly. At last a moment of quiet is upon us. Dog curls himself up tightly on the ground next to me and soon I hear the gentle soughing of sleep coming to him. He's not had the easiest time of it so far here in his new home.

Who are you anyway, Dog, and what were you before? I haven't seen you do one guard dog thing since you got here except bark at trucks and runaway wheelchairs, and you haven't attacked a single person yet even though I've presented you with several good targets. Are you aware, Dog, that the Mexicans are here without permission? Shouldn't you be on that? No, I don't suppose I would be either if I were you. They don't even have a decent roof over their heads there at the increment. You like playing ball with the kids, don't you? I watched you. Is that what they taught you in guard dog school? Maybe you weren't such a great student. I went to school once. I believe I did. All I remember is a lady and a clock on the wall. Or perhaps that was something I saw on the teevee at breakfast. So what was it like, this guard dog school? Did they make you do drills? Did you march and do calisthenics? How was the food? Ever see any action, on someone else's mountain perhaps? I'll bet you said no more of this, didn't you?

If the past must be lost, does it matter what tomorrow brings? Not to you, I heavily suspect. Me neither. The days of our lives are numbered. Any fool can see that. So blessed are the fools who can't count. That's what I believe. It's as plain as the big nose on your face. There's nothing about heaven that doesn't strike me as a bad idea. It seems so unnecessarily complicated, this wanting to exist for all eternity...why? So people can stew about all the things that made them miserable while they were here? Do they expect to forget all about this life, what they did, who they knew, all that they wished they had said or hadn't said? Do they long to have all their moments here in this life erased, just as mine have been erased? Is that what they're really after? If that's what they want then maybe that's what they deserve. I'm sure Lilly wants it. She would buy her way into heaven if she could. I'll bet Otto plans to barge in like he's taking a table at a restaurant. And even though the waitress seems to be of two minds on most subjects, I'm sure she believes the everlasting will sort it all out for her, one way or another. Penzio says no, but I'm pretty sure his problem is that he believes everyone else is going except him. Don't you think, Dog, it all seems a bit desperate? Why can't they see that all this talk about heaven and some lord and whatever what's his name, that preacher man, was screaming about on the big teevee, it's just words for what might be the halfway decent way for people right here in this life to act. The only real problem is deciding if it's worth it to be halfway decent. A fossil, that's my choice. Eons from now, somebody will be digging in the dirt and there I'd be, stuck in a rock or suspended in a sliver of amber, and they'd look at me and go hmm, I wonder what kind of creature this was? Seems halfway decent. And maybe they'd piece me together and put me on display in a museum for everyone to gawk at. Behold, Gustav Man, it would say on a little brass placard, an example of Homo sapiens sapiens, now extinct. They perished from earth clawing their way to eternity.

Perhaps I'm wrong. Perhaps there's no good reason to be halfway decent. Why not take up the mice are stupid method and build yourself a fancy house on the side of a mountain? Drive a fancy car. And live out your fancy days, as many as you may have, thinking that heaven is up there just waiting for you to come along. It's a system, I suppose, like any other system people glom onto to get from one end of things to the other. Law of the jungle and all that. Kill or be killed. Whatever works in the charnel house. Maybe one way is not so different from another. It's all screwing and lamp chops anyway, if the truth be told.

What do you think, Dog? Pretty silly, huh? All these people problems. Is it good to be a dog? Any of that people angst roiling about in that furry noggin? Wish you had yourself a Jesus? Feel bad about not talking on the phone? I doubt it. You don't bother with all that, do you? But I wonder if you don't think life isn't just a little bit miraculous. Have you ever stopped to consider? A bowl of food comes out of nowhere, a ball is tossed where there was none before, an ear is scratched, the head patted, a paw is held until sleep comes, and all without prayer or proffer or the slightest utterance of request. It's just me, Dog, but I am not your Christ. Your hairy self is its own state of grace and there's no obligation to cry out Hey Zeus to catch my attention. I am here for you, Dog. So let's not bother with a name for it. I am here for you and no harm shall come to you as long as I'm around.

And how long shall that be? Well, that's the question, isn't it? Shall we ask the doctors from Tel Aviv? Prognosis is poor in the long run and the long run is growing shorter with every passing moment. So what then of this scrap of time I have right now, here on the edge of the mountain in the first glow of morning? How many scraps compose an era or an epoch? Too few, by my calculations. An eon is but a tick of the clock, the long term a flake of time, and life is a name this human proposes to give an infinitesimally small thing meaning so he'll have some reason to howl at the moon. But no name is needed where there's a ball to throw. No clock is required to chase a common miracle. I am not your lord and master, Dog. I am just a man. It is salvation enough for me.

TWENTY-NINE

It's time to end our retreat and return to the shack. The sun is peaking over the horizon, the cool of these early morning hours has already begun to dissipate and the desert heat is upon us. Both Dog and I are ready to flop.

We round the corner of the pool house and turn back into the yard. With the shack in sight, the dog bolts. Something has caught his eye and he's after it for all he's worth.

When I catch up I discover the source of Dog's personal commotion. A skinny little dog is paying us a visit. I recognize it immediately; that woman, what's her name, the one with the hair.

What it is doing here I don't know. Right now, it's doing it's best to avoid being licked into oblivion by my hairy beast. Dog seems very happy to have some company and the little dog takes the tongue mauling with a practiced resignation. Only when I pull forward and give Dog some stern face does he let up on the poor thing. Dog assumes a sit-at-attention posture directly in front of me, his training I assume, the only thing he apparently remembers from guard dog school. The little dog takes a few moments to give the immediate area a good sniff, but soon joins Dog in posing at my feet, although I doubt any sort of schooling is responsible. More likely, Dog told it to.

The two of them sitting like this, one monster, one midget, waiting for their orders from a mute is good for a smile. Dogs don't tell jokes, but I am beginning to see how funny they can be. Dog is solid at his station. Not a muscle moves. The little one is have trouble with the formation, twitching with an abundance of energy, needing to move, to go. This I assume was learned on the old lady's lap. School of lap. The worst kind.

Perhaps that woman is in the house visiting Lilly. Or maybe that son of hers, Marvelous, Mutton Minor, although I can't imagine what he would be doing here. I suppose I'll have to investigate, but not now. I have two dogs who wish to remind me of some basic biology and the diversity of life. The gene is never satisfied. It wants to herd cattle, but it also needs to sit on the legs of emaciated old women. Is there anything it can't do? I will need to feed these inscrutable genetic bundles very soon, that is obvious.

Was there something in my fridge? I don't recall. The three of us take a look. Dog remembers. When I open up, he seem indifferent. The little one tries to climb inside, and there's plenty of room because there's not a morsel to be had. I'm not sure what I want to do about this. There's a big bag of dog food in the laundry room but the thought of returning to the stone house does not appeal. Dog is doing that sitting thing again. No creature sits more intensely than Dog. You're hungry. I understand. All right, I'll go. Keep your fur on.

Outside once more and I see that the day has already begun for the Mexicans. I catch the first vile fumes of meat searing over their open fire, this breakfast smoke is inescapable. The dogs have caught the scent too and scurry up to the ruins. They are unprincipled and vernal gourmands, not to mention expert beggars, and they score a handout almost immediately. A Mexican steps out from the cavern of the first floor and yells to me, *I feed your dogs, okay? You come too. Good food.*

Rather not, but I do stay put to watch the dogs enjoy the meal, first by the man and then by the children who have made a game of it, giggling wildly as the dogs dance for the dangling treats. In no time the Mexican enclave is buzzing with activity. Items of clothing are stretched on a line across the second floor like so many flags staking claim to the new territory. Some of the women are busy preparing breakfast for everyone, while others are adding and removing clothes from the clothesline, and down below the men gather around a garden hose washing up and chatting amiably. I don't understand a single word they're saying but I can tell they're enjoying themselves. Laughter seems to come easily to these men, and not once do I hear the tone of voice that could be translated as goddamnit.

Up top, out from behind a pair of dangling pants pops Penzio.

Chow, Gustavo, he cries out like he hasn't seen me in eons. The mechanic races down the rickety wooden stairs and runs across the yard towards me.

Hey Gustavo, whaddya know? Penzio stands in the shade by the potting table a little out of breath and lights a cigarette. *Itsa gonna be a hot one today, my friend.*

We pass the interval observing the activity at the increment. I think about these people now occupying the incomplete, unrefrigerated portion of the stone house. I don't know why they've decided to camp here. People have their reasons for doing things that don't always make sense to other people. Maybe two floors with no walls, no roof and no electricity is better than what they had before. Maybe they're just taking up in a place they feel belongs to them anyway. Somehow money must figure into the scheme. It usually does. But there is something else, something basic and fundamental that sticks out for the whole world to see, but I'm not the one to say. People are forced to live in the world together. I live in the gardening shack in the back, out of the way, and I don't understand what is wanted and why is wanted and how come it's all so desperate.

Penzio flicks his cigarette into the shaggy grass and says, *Come, have some breakfast with us. I push you.*

His brisk, determined pace offers no opportunity for objection. When the men see me coming they gather round in a welcoming sort of way. Penzio says something in a foreign language which seems to make them very happy. *Hey ho!* they all cheer, and before I know it they're all following along as Penzio pushes me toward the stairs, and then, somehow, a completely new and unexpected sensation, the men lift me, chair and all, up the stairs and onto the second floor where the others have gathered around the stove fire for their morning meal. I am greeted like some kind of returning hero with more hey hos and pats on the back and big smiles from the women and giggling from the children wanting to touch my chair. I smile too perhaps, although I don't know why. This is the last place I wanted to be this morning. I was going to take a nap. Instead I watch as one of the women prepares some food. Thinking it might be for me, I look at Penzio. He seems to know what I am thinking and says something to the woman. *See see,* she says. *Iz okay.*

Penzio tells me, *Gustavo, I tell her no meat just like you no want. She puts only beans and cheese. You will like this.* Penzio's assurance is no assurance when it comes to food.

The meal is offered on a plate fashioned from aluminum foil. I give this food a good looking over. Something wrapped in something with something poured over the top. And some cheese. An absolute horror. But now that I have it up close I can't say that it smells all that bad. Perhaps it's the cheese. The thing appears to be a real cheese bonanza. So how does one eat this thing? Not a fork in sight and everyone is waiting for me to take a bite, grinning and goading me on like my eating this is going to be the best thing that ever happened. It doesn't seem right that I should be put out by it. After all, I've eaten that stiff-necked oaf Frenchie's food under less than ideal circumstances. I'll eat it, if I can figure out how.

My perplexity must be apparent. The woman who prepared the thing demonstrates for me by miming out the method. I am to wrap the bottom of it in the foil and eat it like a sandwich, with my hands. I follow her instructions as best I can and am not displeased. Its heat is not transferred through the foil which makes it easy to manage while keeping the food steamy hot. There is something brilliant about this. The elimination of table service. My arm is still. Penzio tells me, *Go on, eat...manja.*

I bring it to my lips and take a nibble from a corner. Bready. Very hot.

The Mexicans think very hot is funny. They all laugh and

encourage me to blow on it. *Poof poof,* they demonstrate in unison. I give it a couple of my best poofs and take a real bite. Hmm..not so bad. Like hot cheese and crackers mostly, a bit on the spicy side but not unpleasant. The beans are vaguely pasta-like in taste and texture. I believe this is a meal I can eat. When I smile my satisfaction everyone gets very excited, smiling and laughing, the kids clapping and giggling. And that's that. They go back to doing whatever they were doing before, only Penzio sticks around.

It's good, like I say, eh? It is called burrrr...eato, con kayso ee free holies. Now you are a real Mexican like me too.

Yes, it is good. I eat the thing and enjoy every bite while Penzio talks up a storm.

*You know, Gustavo, these Mexican people they are not so different from Italian people. People is people, like they say. A little like home for me here. The food, maybe is better in Eatalia. But is okay, you know? Okay. Everyone okay but that French...*and Penzio says something in a tone that could be translated as asshole. *Big trouble that French make for me. I like to punch him right in the nose. Maybe I do this. Maybe I get him good. You know, he is here living.* Penzio makes a gesture at a door I am familiar with only from the other side. It was intended to join the rest of the house to the increment. It has always been locked, but no longer. It seems the mechanic has defeated the lock with his tool bag.

I had to do it, Gustavo. Very hot all day. Two women here they are having babies soon. What else I do, eh?

They can use the whole house as far as I am concerned.

Come over here, Gustavo. I tell you something. Penzio leads me over the edge of the structure away from the others. Squatting down to my eye level he says,

I go today. I say goodbye now. Maybe no time later. I want to tell you this. Everybody says you no smart, not right in the head. But I know different. I see what they no see right here in your eyes. Why they no see and I see? Maybe they no want to see. Maybe they too crazy. Maybe they don't know how. A great Italian man say once, the secret to life is to learn how to see. But nobody listen to him right. They think he say learn how to say, so they they talk too much, just like me. Too much talk makes for crazy people, like that maid girl. She is too much crazy. First I think she tries to fool your mama acting she's like one thing, so I test her. I test her real good, I no tell you how, but I test good and for sure I think I catch her, but she no get fooled. How it is, I say to myself, that God he makes a person two people when he makes it hard enough to be one? I think about this a long time, Gustavo. I ask myself the question but no good answer comes. I argue with myself. But no good answer. Then I think, if no good answer comes then maybe the bad answer is the answer. And you know what is the bad answer, eh? The bad answer is God, he is crazy too. He is most crazy of anybody. And all of the sudden I have no more questions. Now I understand. Crazy God, crazy world full of crazy people. And I pray no more. If yes is a God then he knows how to see, I no have to tell him nothing. If he is too crazy then why I pray to him, eh? I am done with pray. But I think about Gustavo and I hope one day he is okay because I think you are a good man. Not crazy like mama and papa. Not crazy like old Penzio. Now is time to go.

I want to tell him...I would say if I could...don't go. Not yet. You've always been halfway decent to me, to the best of my recollection.

Penzio sticks his head between the wooden bars of the increment's cage and takes a long look at whatever is out there, beyond. *Stupeedo house, nice view,* he says, then he leaves, out the door he busted open. In the yard I can see Dog playing ball with the boys on the tennis court. The little dog is there too, barking for all it's worth.

THIRTY

I don't know what to think about Penzio. How he came to be here or when we met, I can't recall. People leave. They come and go around here all the time. What good does it do to try to remember everybody? People leave.

I'd like to take a nap now. I'm full of burrr-eato and I feel like I haven't slept since the last equinox. I want to go home but I can't go down the stairs. The Mexican men are nowhere to be seen. My only option is a poor one; take the door and go through the house. Try not to bump into anyone, the man and the woman being the anyone.

My entrance into the house is a bit on the awkward side. The thresholds don't match up, and in the game of wheelchair matching thresholds is one of the better rules. When I am all the way inside I am hit with a blast of cold air. Penzio was right to bust the lock. It's too hot to be born out there. And beside, no one bothers with this end of the house anymore. Pointless bedrooms full of unneeded, unwanted crap, relics of the un-required, forgotten as fast as they are acquired. All the doors are open, and as I pass I see families, mothers and fathers and little children, on the floor and up on the beds, watching teevee, enjoying the cold air. I hear babies crying. Translation not necessary. The corridor is alive with their chatter. Children are running from room to room playing their games, obeying rules.

As I roll by, the Mexicans smile and wave, glad to see me all over again.

The last door on the corridor is not open. Inside I can hear a teevee and from it a familiar voice. I think about what Penzio said about the French chef and the waitress living up here and how they're responsible for him having to leave. I get mad. I get real mad. And I'm not sure what I'm going to do about it, but I need to do something. So I knock on the door. I knock again, louder. The door opens and it's the French chef, standing in what I'm pretty sure now used to be my room.

You, the chef says. *What?*

I give him what I intend to be my maddest glare.

I am not cooking zee food today. Go home.

I attempt to intensify my mad look. Then I hear the waitress off somewhere yelling, *Jock, who is it?*

The chef yells back, *It is zee boy. He is leaving.*

No, bring him in here. I want to see him.

The door opens wide and with a pissy swish of his hand, the chef motions for me to come in. I try to run over his foot.

The waitress is across the room, wrapped in a towel.

Honey, watch yerself some teevee. I'll be out in a sec.

Apparently, my angry look had little effect on the chef. He drops into a chair and starts reading a book. There's not much I can do about being mad after all. Mad is not my best thing. I should leave. But right then...that voice. On the teevee. I heard it in the hallway. I take a look and there's that guy...from the visit...with the big head...Lambent Hardley. Ha! I remembered his name. And Lambent's on the stage, the one I was on, and there's the big gold chair and stairway to nowhere and...he chose the white roses. That's nice. I decide to watch myself some teevee.

...He was like Socrates, this Jesus. And he went to the people that he might inquire of them the nature of their misery, as he was perplexed and troubled by the depth of their sorrows.

What? he asketh them.

We don't really know, O Lord, they said in concert. We have no good idea what to do about our troubles. What would you do?

And Jesus, long weary of this particular question, said unto his flock, Isn't there something else you would rather ask me?

Like what, Lord? the people wondered.

Well, what's on your mind these days? Just off the top of your head.

And the people replied, We're full of dread and unspecified agitation, savior. What shall we say? Shall we offer you a prayer?

Jesus was becoming impatient with the people. He told them, Don't say anything. Why spoil your every agitation with a prayer?

But Lord, they cried, praying is all we got.

Don't call me that, snapped Jesus. It's just Jesus or Christ, okay? Either one is fine. But not Lord, please. I'm no different from you.

Incredulous, the crowd protested, But are you not the Lord, Prince of Princes, Creator of the Universe, the One who made us?

Jesus sighed mightily, for he knew the great power of a name among the people. Sure, sure. Whatever, he told them. But then, overcome with a great need of his own, brought on by those who would call him Lord and themselves his flock, he rose up to his full measure and said unto them,

Actually, Dad made you. He put me in charge of customer service. If that makes me the Lord, fine. I'll be the Lord. So whaddya need, eh? Step right up and give it to me straight because I've heard all the prayers you can imagine, all the prayers that can be imagined by a coliseum full of professional prayer imaginers a jillion times over, and you'd be amazed at how much they all sound alike after awhile: O Lord, they always begin, my luck's run out. I can't cope. In a real jam here, Jesus. Could use some divine intervention right about now.

Don't get me wrong. I know the score. I know it's tough out there. Not just for you, but for all things that liveth. I've always said that the saddest thing of all is to metabolize. Everything is born with its heart half broken and all too often it's downhill from the get go. But there's no point in mumbling about it to the holy whoisit because, people, the hard facts are that the phone is off the hook up there. The only supreme entity listening to your prayers is located between your ears.

But you need your prayers. I get that too. So let me suggest a prayer for you whenever that special need overcomes and you just have to chat. Try it. It'll help, really. And you can begin it by saying O Lord if you have to. I should be used to it by now. It goes like this: O Lord, please leave me alone. I don't need you right now. I've got troubles, sure, but I don't see how you can help, and besides, you're not all that good at what you do. At this time I could do as well or better without your divine guidance, such as it is. Really, Jesus, I've got this one, but thanks for listening...

Wow, that would be one for the ages. Just one time I'd like to hear you say that. I still love you, understand. More than you know. But you're missing the point. I'm you. You're me. The best and the worst of you. No need to make the distinction, it causes you all kinds of grief. You know what you should do? Try offering yourselves a prayer. What could it hurt? You should say something like this: I am the Lord Mankind, the be all and end all, the bee's knees of real live deities. All the beasts of the mountains and all the creatures of the seas, humble yourselves before me! The birds that flyith and the fish that swimmith, the hapless tuna, the little lamb, prepare thyselves for the dinner plate. Behold Man, ruler of the roost, keeper of the gate, the roughest beast of all! I, Man, who at every moment...at every moment is destroying one and perfecting another christ, and all the while mad, mad, mad for his own demise. Now give that one a shot, and don't forget to say Ah...men.

The waitress comes out of the bathroom in her underwear, a towel wrapped around her head.

I just love that man. He's so...inspirational. Well, looky who's come for a visit. It's Gussie. Hey there, little fella. What's shakin?

Nothing. Remember? She flits around the room getting ready to go somewhere, I assume. That's what suitcases are for, to go somewhere.

Didn't know we was livin' up here, did ya? Us and all them Mexicans. Can you believe it? Why, they're everywhere, ain't they? Jock here can't stand the smell of their food.

It is not food. Do not call zee food food, the French chef says without looking up from his book.

Anyway, we're gettin' outta here on account of...well, shit. Maybe I shouldn't be tellin' ya.

He is idiot boy. Tell him, no tell him. It is zee same.

The laconic cook could have said, Speak, the mute are moot. That is, if he wasn't such a troglodyte. The term boy I will ignore for now. I am not a boy and you are, thankfully, leaving. To forget is to forgive.

Unexpectedly, the waitress comes to my defense on the matter.

He ain't no boy, Jock. No need to be callin' him a boy, she tells him, shaking her finger at his disinterested face. She turns to me and gives me a look over.

How old are ya anyway, hon? Can ya tell me somehow? Hold up yer fingers, make some sign? Can ya write it down? No, yer mama said ya can't write neither. Lordy, honey, bless yer heart, you are fucked up, ain't cha? Hmm...If I had to say...the thing is, yer mama and daddy, they're like ancient sorta, so ya gotta be at least...unless yer mama had you when she was way ripe for it. Ya gotta be...why I'll bet yer 'bout as old as I am. And I'm no tellin' my age cause women don't tell them things. So there.

To which the chef adds, *One idiot talks to second idiot.*

And the waitress replies, *Shut the fuck up, Frenchie.*

Time to flee. I turn my chair and catch sight of some familiar objects in various stages of packaging. I am certain they are pieces from Lilly's fatuous art glass collection, and the one she prizes most of all, the giant glass clamshell, is partially bundled in a bath towel.

As I was sayin', we're gettin' outta here cause...

Money. She's going to say money.

...of money, honey. It takes just one bounced check for this gal. Rich bitch can clean her own toilet.

And cook zee lamb chops. The chef has abandoned his book and is now speeding through the teevee channels like he's trying to compose one enormous program. Uncanny how his head never moves, just the eyes. He's built to watch teevee.

And ya know what else? This is goin' to make ya mad. She comes to me and says, Anna Mary, cause she can't even say my damn name right,

Anna Mary, she says, I'm sufferin'. You have no idea what I'm goin' through. And I says to her, the whole world is sufferin' from one thing or another, lady. Yer just pissed cause yer sheets ain't clean. Pray for my son, she says, all pleadin' and needy like I'd begrudge a poor soul a prayer. Sure, I'll pray for him, I says, and I did too. Didn't we pray together that day? She was watchin', ya know. But I didn' tell her it ain't goin' to do no good. The fact's the facts. Yer goin' to hell there, little guy, and there ain't nothin can be done about it. And that's cause you wasn't baptized. Those are the rules. Get baptized or down ya go. Maybe ya don't care about rules, yer mama bein' a jew and yer daddy bein' a papist and all. Maybe nonna ya care what happens to ya when ya leave this world. But one thing I'll say and ya should be listenin' real good: if ya ever hope to get right, ya oughta be prayin' yerself to the lord every wakin' hour of the day. Ya need to tell him how sorry ya are about everything ya done and how much ya love him and that ya wanna talk and walk and not be a big spazz no more. Sorry to have to talkin' that way but thems the god-honest truth. It's yer mama's fault, ya know. Acceptin' the lord coulda fixed everything. I told her. And besides, a very smart man told me that all ya got is some terrible personality disorder and Jesus can't be fixin' that sort of thing with all the real sufferin' goin' on everywhere. Ya oughta cut it out, ya know what I mean? Yer mama says she don't believe in God. That's the stupidest thing I ever heard. If there ain't no God then who does she think was Jesus' daddy, huh? Answer me that one.

Just then, I catch him. The French chef, noticing that I have spied the cobbled together treasure...and ha! The head turns. I knew it. Not so stiff-necked, after all, you bastard. He gets up from his teevee and comes right up to me.

Listen to me, boy. Maybe you talk, maybe no. I no care. But you see nothing here, are you understanding? You no tell, you no write, you no make little signs with zee fingers. Because if you do this, I make zee promise. You no breathe. I am being clear, yes?

The chef retreats to his teevee chair and I am pleased to retreat my chair out of there.

THIRTY-ONE

BEFORE I COULD POINT old lefty exit-wise, the cops pour in. A veritable hoard of them. Right away, Frenchie throws up his hands, while the waitress scrambles to cover herself. The cops have them red-handed. The booty is in plain sight.

But for some reason, the police don't seem particularly interested in the booty. They turn the place upside down. Drawers are pulled out, closets rifled through, suitcases unpacked. The only thing they don't bother with is the packaging efforts of Lilly's glass collection. It's right there, fellas, I would tell them. The thing that looks like a clamshell. Why aren't you...

I turn my head and there he is, the sheriff. I won't soon forget that bulgy-eyed bastard.

The waitress goes Argentinean. *I think you are not allowed to come in here,* she says in her sweet other voice, *May I see your search warrant, please.*

We're not using them anymore, ma'am. Now everyone stay right where you are, says the sheriff, employing a variation on the more familiar nobody move. Perhaps they're not using that one anymore either.

A certain Penzio, alias the Mechanic, was last seen in this vicinity. He is wanted by local law enforcement on a charge of malicious gate lockin' and by the federal authorities on an immigration warrant. Also, the Eyetalian government is seekin' his extradition on all sorts a violations and criminal contrivances. If you know the location of this individual, you are required by law to speak up.

I can't believe this. These two clown are getting ready to abscond with a load of stolen glassware—granted, it's beyond crap—and you're looking for Penzio? Still with the lock on the gate? And if it's Penzio you want, why are you going through the trash basket?

The sheriff has yet to acknowledge me. He approaches the chef.

Sir, are you acquainted with the suspect?

What do you mean, I am zee one who is telling you about him.

Just answer the question, sir. And put your hands down.

Yes, yes. I know him. He is just out there, on zee building they have not been finishing.

I didn't ask you where he is, I asked if you know him. Now, can you tell me the last time you saw the suspect?

But I tell you, he is there, out zee door. With zee Mexican peoples. You go look.

Was that today?

Yes, yes. Right now. What is your matter? You must go. He will be getting away.

I know my job well enough, sir. Your papers?

I show my papers before. Two times.

Your papers, sir.

The French chef retrieves a card from his wallet and hands it to the sheriff. The sheriff scrutinizes alternately the card and the chef. He says, *Hmm*, then returns the card and walks over to the waitress who is trying cover herself with her little towel. He gives her the once over. He gives it to her again.

Ma'am, he says.

My husband has told you everything, officer. That horrible man is outside. You must hurry.

Ma'am?

As you can see, I do not have my papers on me. I must find them. It is such a mess you have made.

That won't be necessary. I've seen your papers.

The sheriff backs away from the waitress until he is practically on top of me. He quickly swings around.

Ah, Mr. Gustav Arturo. We meet again.

He'll get nothing from me.

Still not talkin', I see. I don't suppose you know where I might find this mechanic fella, do you?

[speechless]

Alright, we'll do it your way. I'll talk and you listen. Fact; we are aware that you are a known associate of Mr. Mechanic, and were last seen not more than an hour ago eatin' a burrr-eato in his presence on these very premises. Also a fact; you have participated in conversations with said mechanic on numerous occasions during which certain subjects of a subversive and anti-democratic nature were discussed, including the details of an incident that took place in an automobile factory located in the former communist country of Yougo-slavia for which Mechanic was arrested, tried and sentenced in the people's court of Eyetalia. But that sentence was never carried out, was it Mr. Gustav Arturo? Because, as you very well know, the suspect escaped incarceration and fled to America. That's felony fleeing, Mr. Gustav Arturo, and your silence on the matter makes you an accessory to that crime. Now, I would very much like to stay and discuss with you the maximum number of years in jail you'd be facin' when we pursue a case against you, and pursue we shall, but right now I have a runaway Eyetalian to catch. I'll be back. You can count on that. Let's go, boys.

The sheriff does not give me an opportunity to run over his foot. He is gone. The French chef and the waitress appear to be having trouble closing their mouths. I can't stay. I must find Penzio.

I choose the highest gear, which for old lefty here is as fast as my arms can fly. My graceful arm steps up to the challenge magnificently. When I zoom past Lilly her voice is distorted by the Doppler effect. My guess is that if he is unable to leave the property, Penzio will head for the garage. I make it to the elevator, but when I push the down button nothing happens. I push again. Broken. Everything's broken in this crap house. Goddamnit.

I head for the stairs. Clinging to the railing, I slide myself down most carefully and with great effort, my legs humming their protest over this exercise of unexpected excess. But having navigated the treacherous decline, I realize my impulsive choice of paths through the labyrinth of the stone house has left me without a means of locomotion, to wit; I'm stuck at the bottom of the stairs, chairless. I test my legs. A sensation of thin juice, aware that I am of some capacity, waxing and waning as it does, less according to need than to luck, or the temporary cessation of syndromatic tendencies. A little help, as they say in the game of ball, would be useful about now, and I spy at the front door a stand of umbrellas, a cache of canes. One particularly sturdy number serves the purpose and I, intrepid gimp that I am, hobble through the laundry room and exit the house and onto the drive.

No cops in sight. They must still be searching the house, hung up, no doubt, combing through the superabundance of powder rooms. No Penzio in sight either, and I stop not far from what is left of the horsehead fountain to rest my legs. It's pointless, I suppose. There is nothing I can do for Penzio that he can't do for himself right now. Fleeing is a personal project more often than not, and there is rarely time during the act to acknowledge the peripheral gesture of moral support, however well-intentioned. I am not unfamiliar with the dynamics of the good getaway; run hard, keep your head down, don't look back, don't stop to say hey ho to every wellwisher along the way. I just hope Penzio has the practiced good sense to follow these simple rules. The sheriff says I am complicit, an accomplice to a litany of offenses too absurd to contemplate—turn the screw, lost in the world, seeing not saying—too absurd to imagine, even for a coliseum full of absurdity imaginers. That's one edifice that will never go unoccupied, to be sure. In the game of Homo sapiens, that arena will always be packed to the rafters. Not even the syndromatically disconnected are excused from attendance.

I hear a rumble and a grumble erupting out the maw of the underground garage, and up the ramp comes Penzio, driving my birthday car. He sees me and stops.

I know what you think. English piece of shit, but I fix good. No poof. I must hurry now, Gustavo. You are a good man and my friend. Take care of that dog of yours. He is a good boy. Remember, be careful what you believe. This is a crazy world for everyone. Chow, Gustavo!

The mechanic speeds away, around the rubble of the horsehead fountain and down the drive. The car sputters and crackles under the hard charge of intrepid fleeing, and I suppose Penzio believed the operation he performed on the two halves of the gate would allow him to pass without protest, or perhaps he forgot they can be opened manually with the turn of a crank, but the act of fleeing sometimes clouds one's memory to such things. The gates do not yield. They gather up the jungle cat in its torn but otherwise impenetrable net and crumple it up like a wad of aluminum foil. A loud crack, not so much a poof as a bang, echos through the canyon and a thick gray cloud of smoke rises over the desiccated treetops. The cops hear this too and a bunch of them rush by me to converge on the wreckage. Not too close, though, because of the flames.

Pretty soon I hear sirens coming up the mountain road, and more quickly than I would think possible the commotion is cleared away to make way for the catering trucks.

THIRTY-TWO

An army of waiters and waitresses has descended upon the stone house, an invasion force of table servers clad in white, come to prepare for the big party. Trucks loaded full of tables and chairs. Others full of forks and spoons. I catch a ride on a cart stacked with potted palms and end up on the east patio where no breakfast is being served at the enormous glass top table. Otto is here now, wild-eyed and unshaven, at table's head, his place closest to the view. He is surrounded by his business buddies who are no less the worse for wear. All that rhyming has really taken its toll. This is a group seriously in need of a nap. Also at table, the most southern portion of it, naturally, is a small contingent of Mexicans from the increment. They have taken control of the teevee remote and are enjoying a program in their native language starring a man and a woman drinking coffee. I stay out of sight, but I doubt Otto would bother to notice me. He's still heavily in poem mode and he's declaiming up a storm.

Now let us speak of paradise and all that is beautiful to us. Shall beauty be the rose whose blossom withers, never to be refreshed? Shall this beauty be a sapling stalk, torn of its roots by an unchaste hand? Must we call it paradise all that by a petulant grief cannot abide a golden ray or the glad tidings of a prosperous spirit? Or, shall we wield the word like a silver'd sword and cut upon the impudent persuasion of the meek, the merciful, the feckless of heart, the burdened overly, the trodden downwardly, the taxed unfairly until all things known by a name shall be known by another? If beauty be in the beholder's eye, then behold the eye of this beholder! I spy with my mighty eye a revelation which neither monstrous love nor the faithless kind dare recalculate to a lesser preference. To me, upon my mountain, a truth most famous has been delivered which I do proclaim; that all men are created...unequal!* He bangs his handkerchiefed hand on the table, recoiling in pain. *Goddamnit! Who do I have to screw to get a cup of coffee around here?*

One of the Mexicans, taking note of his distress, crosses the table's length with a big red thermos and fills his cup. Otto takes a sip. *Hmm...that is good coffee,* he says. *Grassy us,* replies the Mexican, but when he tries to return to his seat Otto grabs him by the shirt. Now Otto is addressing the Mexican.

A vision has come to me. This, the site of our all too brief habitude, brought forth by dint of will and indelicate persuasion, shall some day hence decry the reckless scheme and cast off these lowly schemers. With slabs of stone upon their backs and strapped like chastened beasts they will slog and toil beneath a witless sun for what crusts we may afford them and nevermore conjure a thought of our demise nor receive from us what is sacred. O, Glorious, our ascension to this sublime currency whose affection for us exceeds a natural tendency....

The Mexican pulls free of Otto's grip and returns to his place at the other end of the table. All the Mexicans give Otto a dirty look as if to say, next time get your own coffee. But fiery Otto will not be put down. He turns to his business buddies, a weary, haggard, uncomplaining lot who haven't slept, who never even got the meal they were promised.

Did I mention that money loves me? She really loves me. Every night I give it to her good and come morning she begs for more. And there's nothing she won't do for me, but I tell her, try as you might, you only have one nose. Money doesn't mind. Why should she? Without me money is nothing. Here, I just made a poem about her. It goes like this: She was a fair princess, no longer fair. She was a fair whore, tho' rarely bare. She was a fare princess, after the fall. She was a fare whore, but aren't they all?

This sends Otto into a fit of hysterical laughter. The business buddies are not moved by Otto's doggerel, however. One of them seems to have lost consciousness. *There's no sleeping here!* screams Otto.

I slip unnoticed from the scene and hobble myself shackward, grateful for the umbrella that now serves as my crutch. Party preparations are in full swing. Around the pool and down at the tennis court the white uniformed crew are setting up tables and chairs and stringing lights from the trees and building a stage for the band. Their urgent scurrying tells me that there's not much time left. I have to get some sleep before sleep will be impossible.

I spot Dog and the little dog down there too. They're helping out. They've got themselves a tablecloth and are tearing it to shreds.

All is quiet at the increment. I put myself down and dream a dream of me...

...I am walking on the edge of the world where an endless ocean laps at my side. The sand is cool and soft, conforming, pushing up between my toes, wrapping around my feet as if to say never leave. But day is done. The sun has begun its reluctant descent to the horizon and the ceaseless slopping of the waves informs my own rhythm as I take a line where the sea licks at the earth's dry crust to accommodate my destination. One more breath, this ancient air, more delicious than any meal, having traveled from foreign shores just to fill my weary chest and clear my head and make me right for what is surely coming.

Not yet. Something else first. Something desired.

And I see him running towards me, my rough beast. His motion is pure and unrestrained, as harmonious with the world as the wind itself. He has come to play, and when he gains me the offer of a pat on the head will not contain him. He bounds into the water leaping headlong to capture a wave in his teeth and give it a good shake.

Then out, onto the beach again running wild circles round me, barking his pure, un-divine laugh, and I begin to laugh too. Yes! Yes! What unknown joy! What absolute perfection! And I laugh, because of everything, for all that was done and will be done again and again. I laugh for the words that were spoken and the stories that are told to explain it all away. I laugh as big as the ocean for the trouble they cause one another, for the abuse they heap on those they love and the injuries inflicted on those they don't, for the scars they carry and the veil of trauma worn by the entire human race. I laugh a mad, unholy laugh at time itself, that imperious zealot, that makes fools all the more foolish for the attention they pay it. No more. I shall quit you all soon enough and be done with you forever. But not you, sweet friend. I am with you. You be the one. Lead me away from here, this clumsy world. Show me the way home.

It appears I have been invaded by the Continental Congress. A noisy gaggle of partiers has burst into my shack, my private abode, costumed according to a scheme, curly white wigs and fancy clothes. The men are dressed in half pants, long tailed coats, frilly shirts and clunky shoes with big buckles. The women wear big shiny dresses of blue and white. They have come to admire my lawnmower.

I scan the room for a ride, but nothing, only the umbrella cane recently brought into service to support my syndromatic self. Startled to see me, they babble in unison their apologies for the intrusion. *Awfully sorry, old man...had no idea you were here...just leaving.* And happily, they begin to file out the door. One of the men stops long enough to say, *Oh yes, it is a glorious Fourth of July. It is a great day. It is a good day. God bless it. God bless you all.*

This may develop into a difficult evening. The music coming up from the tennis court is unbearably loud, and even from my relatively sheltered location I can already hear the cackle of a woman whose laugh is heard above all others. Surely, I must flee. But to where? I doubt there is a single corner of the castle that is unoccupied by these fake colonists. For a moment I consider the garage, but then I remember about Penzio, and the thought no longer appeals. Besides, there's a teevee down there and I suspect they'll be all over that as well. Think, Gustav. The private place behind the tennis court wall is too far a walk. If my umbrella were to fail me I'd go right over the edge of the precipice, and not even Dog's barking would summon help. Where is Dog anyway? Fled, smart fellow. I could use my electric chair right about now. I suppose I'll have to go searching for it, out there, in that melee.

I pass the increment. The stove fires have been extinguished, the radios turned off, and the Mexicans are hunkered down like they're expecting a hurricane to strike. Everywhere else the party is in full swing. As I approach the east patio I hope I will be able to slip into the house unmolested, but it is not to be. No sooner do I clear the corner when a be-wigged and fancy tailored man is beside me.

Well, hello there, young man. Remember me?

I do in fact remember the elder Hardley. I can't seem to avoid him.

Hey, look at you. Up and around I see. Feeling better, are we? That's terrific. Say, I'm glad I bumped into you. Wanted to apologize for the other day. I guess we gave you a bit of a rough time. Hope we didn't do any permanent damage.

Lambent looks at me like he half expects me to answer. I don't know what I would say to him except that I look forward to forgetting about it, and that I need to sit down somewhere. I lean up against to wall of the house.

You know, that little show was performed as a favor to someone I never refuse. My intentions were the very best, I assure you.

Yes, yes. I know all about Lilly and her therapeutic machinations. But how is it that you can't refuse her?

When Young Lamb suggested to me that some tabernacle and brimstone might just be the thing to pop you out of your shell I was skeptical at first. Too brute a force, I said. That stuff is made for teevee which softens up the punch. Never liked doing the thing face to face. But he was very persuasive as usual. Anyway, good to see you up and about. Come, sit at our table. Have a drink, something to eat.

When I make a move to flee I stumble and Lambent takes my arm. *I've got you,* he says. He won't stop talking.

The thing is, your old man and I are in the same business, essentially, that is, all commerce seeks out the imbalances, the weaknesses, strengths, advantages, disadvantages, so forth. It's the nature of the world, am I right? I offer people a chance to feel halfway decent about themselves. If I can stave off the common existential dread, who would fault me for that? Best thing a person can do for another person when you come right down to it. A few bucks here and there for a little hope, some peace of mind. Why, they're glad to pay. And besides, we're all adults here. We all exercise our free will, do we not? Of course, the difference between your father and me is that your father is a complete psychopath. Perhaps you've noticed. Sheep and mice, that's what he thinks of his fellow human beings. And what's with the rhyming? All that rhyming...mooney, spoony, doony. I heard him say that the other day. What the hell is dooney, for godsakes? A babbling lunatic, if you ask me. A clown, and a dangerous one too. He'll cut your heart out and not think twice about it. Yep, a real sociopath and bent, completely.

Lambent is relentless in his yammering as he leads me to the enormous glass top table. At first I don't recognize anyone. Their get-ups are pretty much alike, founding fathers and mothers. There's a couple of Otto's business buddies at the far end all wigged up, still in their blue suits. Next to them a few intrepid Mexicans have joined the festivities. I can't imagine where they got a hold of their wigs. And at the head of the table, giving me the eye, is the Vice President of the United States, made up as the President of the United States. I know this because it's pretty much the first thing he tells me.

There he is, the hero of the republic, come to offer his commander some tactical advice. Have a seat right next to me, young man.

Lambent deposits me next to the Vice President and takes the seat opposite me. The Vice President looks like an old woman in his silly costume.

Where's your uniform, soldier? Didn't you read the instructions? You're supposed to be in uniform. I'm Washington, of course. Always wanted to be Washington. Kind of a role model of sorts. And the padre here is what...Paul Revere?

One if by land, two if by sea, offers Lambent.

Yep, helluva shindig your folks put together here. Why, we're all better off for a little unrestrained indulgence, eh?

There's no denying that. Lilly went all out. She's considered every detail: the food, the booze, waiters and waitresses galore, all decked out in what one must assume is period waiting garb. Flags and fanfare are everywhere, hanging from the roof, from the trees, floating in the pool. The red, white and blue-ishness of it all is a remarkable achievement for a woman who can't make up her mind what bracelet to wear in the morning. She's even got a fife and drum corps marching around the tennis court competing with the electric boom-booming of the band. It's quite a show. In another life she might have actually done something.

As impressed as I might have been at that moment with Lilly's finesse for fun, the urge to leave is utmost on my mind. I try to make my move but the Vice President's fat paw grabs me by the arm and sits me right back down again.

I'll order you bound and gagged, sir! Stick around. Dinner's coming.

Have me bound if you will, I would tell him, but I come pre-gagged. At that moment the waiters descend on our table laden with plates and plates of bloody lamb chops. I shake my head violently, doing my best to wave them off. A plate of chops is placed in front of me and the neural synapses have no trouble sending the message to my graceful arm, but the Vice President maintains his grip, one of those ostensibly affectionate, untempered, old mannish sort of clutches that can render even the autonomic nervous systems inoperative, and I am confronted with the twin horrors of lamp chops and table service with no way to respond. Washington proves to be a remarkably strong man for his age, and it is not until my own arm quiets that he relaxes his hold on me. Soon enough, the urge to send the thing flying across the lawn passes, at least for the moment, and my chief concern now is not throwing up on the star spangled tablecloth. I make one more attempt to bolt, but the clamp is quick, and I resign myself to my captivity and wait for an opportunity to present itself.

Looks yummy, he says. The sound of the word from this white wigged old geezer makes my head spin.

The Mexicans begin to mumble a prayer over their plates. *Poor sots,* says Lambent. Does he mean sleeping in bus stations and the other poor sots losing their fins?

Nothing wrong with that, says the Vice President. *Seems to me they have the right idea. Be awfully nice if you'd say grace for us, reverend.*

Lambent has already stuck a fork in his food and seems put out by the request. *I don't know if that's necessary. After all, it's a party...*

Vice Pres: *Grace, Padre! If you please. You people down there, quiet.*

Lambent: *Let's see...Oh lord, keep us in ignorance that we may proliferate in a slow world and deliver us from the exigencies of consciousness.*

Vice Pres: *What a minute here. What kind of goddamn grace is that?*

Lambent: *I haven't finished. Let me thank him for the meal.*

Vice Pres: *No. I don't want you to finish. You've said enough. I've heard talk that you were some kind of heathen preacher.*

Lambent: *If one of us is a heathen, then we both are.*

Vice Pres: *I'm not on your wavelength, sir. It's a scam artist who'd preach one thing and practice another.*

Lambent: *That sound as much a description of your former trade as it does mine.*

Vice Pres: *Bullshit.*

Lambent: *I shall leave it to you then to decide who is the kettle and who is the pot.*

Vice Pres: *That kind of fancy talk might dupe your claque, Hardley, but it doesn't fly with me. Let me show what real table grace sounds like.*

Lambent: *Please, be my guest.*

Vice Pres: *Let us bow our heads. Dearly beloved, we are gathered together on this glorious day to celebrate the birth of our country, best there is, better than all the rest, to give thanks for this meal we are about to receive, for the many splendid entrees and appetizers and the* excellent salad bar. We are all enjoying ourselves very much which I'm sure is what you'd want us to do.

Lambent: *You're talking to God like he's the one hosting this party.*

Vice Pres: *Padre, if you don't mind. Lord, we thank you for all your hard work on our behalf and for being so holy about everything. It makes us holy just thinking about how holy you are, because we Americans are holy people, just fighting to stay holy in a world full of criminals and...*

Lambent: *...and heathens. Don't forget heathens.*

Vice Pres: *Padre, you've interrupted me twice now, and I only interrupted you once. So next time, it's my turn to do the interrupting, agreed?*

Lambent: *Good rule. Proceed with your speech.*

Vice Pres: *Not a speech, sir. A prayer. You might know the difference. Not that I am opposed to the speechifying of prayer, or the prayerification of speech, for that matter. Damn it, I lost my train. Let's see...your tired, your poor, your huddled masses...no, that's that other thing. Didn't care much how that turned out. Should have stuck with just the yearning and worked the rest out in court. Wording is everything, I suppose. But my point is, Jesus, we're thankful for the good table service down here, so maybe all those poor are working out just the same. Part of your divine plan, no doubt. We won't be pressing the matter. Also, your majesty, we're grateful for all the other things, the purple mountains, so forth and so on. Well done. Very attractive, nicely presented. I always try to find time to stop and smell your flowers, especially the yellow ones. Those are my favorite. So, in closing, thanks again for all the holiness. With liberty and justice for all. God bless America. Amen.*

Lambent: *Couldn't have said it better myself.*

Vice Pres: *Kind of you to say, sir. Now let's eat, goddamnit. Wait, I dropped my fork. Waiter...boy, here!*

When the Vice President bends down to retrieve the errant utensil I bolt. But in my haste I bolt to the left (must be thinking about that chair) and am obliged to navigate the partiers poolside.

The pool deck is packed with all manner of Washingtons and

the like, as well as a large mob bedecked in period unspecific bathing costumes frolicking in and out of the water. There's nothing like wet to force the frolic out of a human being. They are a giddy, noisy lot to be sure, and it is all I can do to twist and slide my way around them. Wherever it is that I am going, it cannot be here. I've got to find my way back, but my legs...my legs are so weak and I feel...I think I'm going down...a chair, somewhere...I need a...and down I go, not altogether, but to one knee and right in front of some girl sitting next to the chair I was aiming for. She is wearing, ever so slightly, a bathing suit, and when I look up my eyes meet her significant bosom straight on.

Rise, sir knight, she says playfully, but I cannot. I think she is a little drunk. It's quite possible she thinks I am too. When I fail to stand up or speak or redirect my gaze, her tone changes to something less jocular.

Hey, fella. What's the big idea?

A man sitting at the same table says, *He wants to propose.*

Another man says, *I think he likes you.*

Another adds, *I think he likes them.*

Then someone else says, *It's their kid. You know, the one that's a little, you know.*

The buxom bathing suit girl changes her tone once again. *Oh, yea. Right. Come here, sweetie. Sit right next to me.*

If I were able to get up, I'd leave. For the moment I cannot get up. When I can, I will not need to sit. I will be somewhere else.

He doesn't want to sit by you, says one guy.

The view's better down there, says another.

Sure he does, the girl says. *Right here, darlin'. Come on. I'm Cindy. What's your name again, Gottlieb, Igor?*

They say he doesn't talk. He only says yes and no.

Is that right, sugar? Just yes and no? Can you say yes for me? C'mon, give me a yes.

Maybe you're not his type, suggest the guy.

Show him your tits, suggests another.

I'm not going to show him my...don't listen to these nasty old boys. *Tell me, sweetie pie, is your daddy around here somewhere? You can just shake your head or wave or whatever it is you do.*

Actually, I haven't seen either one of them, which is very odd. It isn't like Otto to vacate the stage for very long. And Lilly, shouldn't she be out here yelling at the help?

I gather my strength, and with aid of the umbrella hoist myself up and away from this commotion.

The only path available to me now is the worst imaginable, through the tennis court, the eye of the storm. Down below, everyone is either dancing or eating or standing around watching one another drink. And they're talking, of course. It's like listening to all the teevee channels at once. I think my brain is going to burst. Then I feel a hand on my shoulder and I think, no more. I turn around and it's Samson. Young Lamb.

Hey, old man. It's me.

Yes, it is you. I remember you, don't I? I've been doing a lot of remembering lately. Of everyone here, he looks most like a doorman.

I've been looking for you. Great party, eh? Looks like you're getting around pretty good there. That's great. Listen, awfully sorry about that little thing Dad and I hit you with, you know, in the studio. Kinda rotten, in a way. We both feel just lousy about it. But who knows? Tough love and Jesus. That's what Dad does best.

Yes, but love was never the question, never the answer.

We did a little something after that, something Dad wanted to do for awhile now. This one's for Gustav, he said. You should try to catch it. Been on the God channel all day. Anyway, let's just forget it, shall we? Lilly, I mean your mom, asked me to come fetch you. She has something she wants to talk to you about. But first, I told my own mom I'd bring her a cookie. She's in a bad way. Lost that dog of hers. Just up and disappeared, the little yapper. Don't half blame it, the way she smothers it like she smothers everything. Monstrous to watch, really. Maybe you know what I mean.

Maybe I do.

I went out looking for it, or that's what I told her. I went golfing instead. Got back all sweaty like I searched real hard. Great game, golf. You should give it a go sometime. Lin Wee's the one who'll have to do the finding. She won't let up on him until he does.

Right about now I'd like to know where those two dogs are hiding out so I could join them. I wonder what Lilly wants. No chance it involves tuna.

On the bench by where the net usually goes, looking more like crumpled tissue than ever, sits the Hardley woman, what's her name...Able, Actual, Agile, Anal, Ankle, Anthill...I can't dig it out. But then, something else, what just happened, something I may have done from long ago in the arrangement of my thoughts, an ordering or sorts that for a moment felt weirdly right. I try to grab hold of the idea, but in all the chaos...and it's gone. Goddamn parties.

I am of two minds regarding the old lady and her lost dog, and I don't feel bad about not going up to her and standing around while she tells me how broken up she is about losing it. The little dog is fine, I would tell her. Off somewhere with Dog staying sane, no doubt, and certainly not pining over the manic pawing it's missing by not being on your lap. But I know you want it back, that you probably care for it more than the two Lambs put together, and until it comes home you'll never be whole again. I'd tell her that if I could. I almost feel I could.

Nevertheless, the cookie is delivered and the old lady, Ample, offers me a flaccid wave and a sad smile. Lamb junior takes a moment with his mother, crouching down all full of phony sympathy, then gives her a kiss on the cheek and we are off again. Maybe he does feel something like grief for her as he doesn't speak again until we get to the house where he mutters something about loss or the redemption of the spirit, more of his father's palaver, and not for my benefit, I'm sure. It's obvious the giant Lamb is trying to be good. On the way to wherever it is we're going I am obliged to stop and rest, and the man is decent about waiting for me to recover my strength. But his big, wiggy, solicitous self makes me uncomfortable. I press on despite these weary limbs.

Into the house through the kitchen, abuzz with unimaginable activity, we arrive finally at the elevator. I recall the thing is broken and give Lamb a look. He pushes the button and car begins to move. *Loose wire,* he informs me. *Took me thirty seconds.* So, it's the garage. The elevator completes its slow descent and the door opens to an empty, hollow place. Not a single car in sight, not even the one thrown in. Lilly is sitting on the edge of the sofa with her back to a dark and silent teevee screen. She is red-uniformed and I can hear her fidgeting as I approach.

You go, Lamb tells me.

With my umbrella cane I give a sure stride my best effort. The motor chair is parked in front of her. She says to me, *You're walking good today. That's wonderful. Come. Sit by me. I want to talk to you.*

I take up the familiar chair. She's been crying. Leaning forward, she gathers my hands together on my lap and holds them firmly. The words don't come to her right away, but soon enough she begins. *Gussie, your father and I...oh dear, I want to tell you something. It's very hard.*

Pull yourself together and concentrate.

For a long time now, Gussie, your mother has not been a very happy person. I've felt alone and desperate like the whole world was coming down on me and there was nothing I could do to stop it. When people feel this way, trapped with no way out, they sometimes do bad things, wrong things. Things that make no sense later on. But I'm not a bad person, Gussie, you know I'm not. I've always tried to be a good mother, haven't I? Oh, why won't you answer me anymore? You're slipping away. I can't bear it any longer.

She squeezes the knot she has made of my hands.

Life is so complicated, so many twists and turns, and you never get to take hold of any single moment and make it your own before it slips right between your fingers. I'm not brave like you. Life frightens me. All I ever wanted was to be happy. It seems like such a simple thing. I believed once I could be happy with your father. But you know how that is. You know as well as anyone, don't you? I thought this house would change things for us. How silly of me. I never liked this house. I never wanted for you to live in the guest cottage, away from your father and me. What I wanted was a home, at long last, so we could live, just live. We are all so full of wants, aren't we? When I was a little girl I wanted to be a dancer. I'll bet you didn't know that about me, did you? I used to love to dance. Remember how you and I danced in the kitchen? You were such a beautiful little boy. We had such fun, you and me. And how we would get in the car and go for a ride in the country and all the wonderful things we saw just driving around? I hope you remember. I wish I knew what was going on in that head of yours. I wish you could talk to me again. All the doctors in the world with their big words and worthless cures. All the fretting, the sleepless nights, the fights with your father. Want to hear something funny? I even tried praying, to Jesus. Yes, funny, eh? The girl, the maid from wherever she's from, showed me how. I got down on my knees and put my hands together like you're supposed to...my mother would spin her grave. I prayed for you to be whole again. Maybe I didn't do it right. Maybe I made things worse.

    She pauses to sniffle and gather herself for what I hope will be a push to the end.

    I don't know what's going to happen to your father. He's made a huge mess of everything like he always does. And he may have to go to jail. I'm just not cut out for this. I can't be the good mother anymore. And so, my dear, sweet...oh, I won't call you a boy. You haven't been a boy for a long time. I'm going to slip away. Tonight. Please don't be sad.

    She starts to cry. A handkerchief is offered to her from behind. It's Lamb the Younger and he's changed out of his party gear. So that's it. She's running away with the preacher's son. He'll be the one driving the getaway car.

    We've found you a nice place where they'll take good care of you. I want you to try to be happy too. I've got to do this, Gussie, (and turning her gaze upward to boyfriend) *we've got to. I'm in love. Can you understand? How I wish you could. I'll never stop believing that one day you'll be well and whole and the man you ought to be, and that you and I can be together again. Someday we'll have ourselves a good laugh over all of this. Promise me, Gustav. Please. Promise. Oh hell, I've ruined my makeup.*

    She tends to her face with the hanky provided by her new fella. I suppose I should be angry with her, sticking me away in some ward to finish out my days while she takes up with a golfer. But I am not mad. I'm not even surprised. I always thought she would leave. On more than one occasion I preferred the thought, although my perfect scenario had Otto going too. I have to admit, in a long life of talking, she has never been more articulate. Misery has a way of conjuring the poet out of just about anyone. And I don't for a minute believe she'll be happy running off with this new oaf. After all, she's heard him play the piano, and I'll bet she's packed more than a few red dresses. I would tell her that happiness is not the thing to aspire to. People find their way to happiness no matter where they are, in jail, or even at death's door. Weeds will continue to intrude on your perfect scheme. But maybe one day you'll know a little peace of mind. If you want to call that happiness, go right ahead. I would also tell you that you were never the parent. That was my job, from in here, where I reside. Letting go is what a parent ought to do. So go.

THIRTY-THREE

I watch the two of them walk up the ramp and out of sight. I don't expect to see her again. She's found herself another bald walrus and she says it's love. Yes, mother, life is complicated. So full of wants.

The garage seems smaller to me now without the cars, more pointless than ever. Maybe the Mexicans will take it up. Nothing useful should go unused.

I put the chair in gear, but nothing. Loose wire. More broke crap. No matter. I don't feel like sitting in the damn thing anyway. It will be dark soon and through the big window I can see the first signs of a fireworks show. A hard, concussive thud is followed by a spray of yellow and red. And another, red and blue. Like potting flowers. I think about the dogs. If they're not frightened by what has already happened today, this will shake them up for sure. I'm going to find them and maybe the three of us will have some cheese and crackers. I press the elevator button to the first floor and watch the car climb right past the first floor and stop at the second. I press it again. No response. The thirty second cure did not take. I am obliged once again to use the stairs. But before I can make that first treacherous step I spot something very strange through the half-open door of the masters' bedroom. It looks like the waitress, sitting there on the floor, and she doesn't look at all comfortable. It's an inexplicable impulse that leads me toward her, and when I push the door fully open I see Otto.

Captain, glad you could make it. Got a couple of prisoners here, sir, but they're not talking. Goddamn guineas. What do you think we should do about them?

The waitress and her husband are sitting in the floor all tied up, propped against the wall. Otto has gagged the chef with what looks like the girl's little white hat, and around her mouth he's tied the bloody handkerchief he's been using to bandage his wounded hand.

Waiting for your orders, Captain. Looters. Caught 'em red-handed. Ha! Red-handed, get it? He sticks his foul, grisly hand in my face. It is full of infection and smells awful. *Seems to me there's only one way to deal with this garbage. Know what I mean? Huh? What's the matter there, soldier, cat got your tongue? A simple yes will do? Hmm. We could throw them to the lions, but I say we give the lions a rest. Don't want any tired lions. Say, I've got an idea.*

With his good hand, his gesturing hand, he removes a pistol from his jacket pocket.

Field execution. By the book. As ranking officer I think you should be the one to carry out sentence.

Otto tries to place the gun in my hand, and he's not delicate about it.

Here, goddamnit. Take it.

My graceful arm snaps and the awful thing goes flying across the room.

Oh Captain, my Captain, what a fuckup you are. First rule of combat, soldier. Hang on to your weapon. But then, combat was really never your thing, was it pissy pants? A little action and you go all moron on us. Isn't that right, papa? Well, never mind. Thank God there's one real soldier on the line.

Otto retrieves the pistol and begins to pace the way he does, caged jungle cat-like, tight and wild-eyed. The gun swinging about at the end of his one good hand fills the room with a horrible dread, but there's no fleeing this time. He's taken his prisoners, the three of us, and it's clear to me it's a conclusion he seeks, some once and for all thing that has always lurked beneath the chaos of his nature. It occurs to me that of all the people I have encountered in this life, of those who have managed to retain a place in my memory, it is Otto I know best.

People leave, he begins. *They leave all the time. So what's to be done? Don't say you're sorry. I don't want to hear some sobby blobby story about how sorry you are, how disappointed you feel about everything, the world you think you deserve. The world, the world, my kingdom for the world. Don't tell me about your goodness, your noble sentiments, how helpful you've been. No one helps me. No one knows how to help me. All they do is take, take, grab, and plunder my wealth for themselves, and expect I'll stand idly by, happy to do their chores, work the field like some goddamn wetback and not even a bicycle to show for it, and I'm supposed to do unto others and believe in the lord as he does unto me. Well, money is my church, I'm here to say, and I've done my penitence. I'll be goddamned if I'm going to carry this house around on my back. And when they realized that I wasn't going to love them they stopped loving me. So go. Leave. Who needs you. Everybody leaves. No point getting all teary about it, is there honey? Why, you're going off to see your Jesus. What fun! Let's have ourselves a party. Sing a song. Here, I'll start you out...Better not scream, better not whine, better not want what oughta be mine, cause Otto Clause is coming to town...What? You don't like that one? Wrong holiday, huh? Well, let's try another. How does that one go...la, la, la 'tis of me, sweet land of liberty...*

Otto points the gun and fires once at the French chef. Blood gushes from his throat.

...for me I sing. Oh, yes. That's a good one. Land where my father tried...

He fires again, striking the waitress in the center of her forehead.

...land where the pilgrims lied. You're not singing, people. I thought for sure this would be a musical bunch. I'm very disappointed. What do you think, Captain? Prisoners won't sing. Shall we offer them some additional encouragement? What's that you say? Yes? Right away, mein fuhrer!

Otto fires several more times into the inert bodies.

Mission accomplished, Commander. And now, it pains me to

bring it up, but there's the matter of your own personal conduct under fire. Cowardice in theater cannot be tolerated, now can it, boy?

Otto turns the gun on me and click.

Out of ammo. How trite. Hang on, I've got more.

He digs into his jacket pocket with his gory hand. Certainly I could flee, so why won't my legs move? As Otto reloads his gun an image flickers on the tv screen in my mind. A child, running in the yard, laughing, and a man, laughing too, chasing, throwing a ball. Like a single photograph spilled from a box over and over again the image comes, time stuck on itself, and it doesn't matter whether I see the honest memory that has chosen to return to me at this moment or the casting of players in yet another fitful dream, I shall allow myself this belief: I was that child. He was that man. And once, long ago, we were somebody else.

Otto raises his pistol. He is most resolute. I give him my best smile. Well, that's that. The last huff huff of conclusion. I've done my deed. It's all archeology from here on out. But then, out of nowhere, bounding into the room, a black blur, and in a single magnificent leap Dog flattens the man as though he were made of tissue paper. The bed obscures my view. I can hear a fierce growling and gnashing and a few muffled groans. A hand is raised, the gesturing hand, and lowered. The dog emerges from behind the bed like it was nothing at all, a bit of mess about his whiskers. He paid attention in school after all.

As fast as my legs will carry me is not a thought I frequently entertain, but it is with unexpected speed that I leave the scene of Otto's horrific crime and seek an exit. The stairs prove no obstacle. I slide down the banister, Dog following right behind, and we're out the door and onto the patio before I realize I no longer have my umbrella cane. It is only out of habit or the racing of my heart that I take the first chair I spot, a vacancy at the glasstop table, one of many as the partiers have gathered at the edge of the precipice to watch the firework show.

Dog doesn't care much for the noisy performance. I don't pay much attention to it myself as dusk has turned to dark and the bright display of exploding rockets recedes against the cataclysm swirling through my brain. I think it would be a good thing if I were able to talk right about now. Somebody should be notified about the carnage that took place upstairs. Hey, everybody, I would shout, shots have been fired. People are dead. Quick. Hurry. But then, what for? I doubt anyone heard the gunfire over the commotion that is taking place in the sky above us. Oddly above us. Directly above us. Suddenly, with every burst of red, white and blue a cascade of sparkling embers begins to fall like the onset of a summer shower over the congregation of fake founders, oohing and aahing with outstretched hands. Dog seems more concerned about the implications of this impractical aiming and takes shelter under the table. I reach down to offer a reassuring pat on the head and see that the little dog has joined him, quivering as though it were sitting on Ample's lap. It's okay, fellas, I would tell them. Just people having their noisy fun. But I have to admit I don't care for it either and maybe under the table isn't such a bad idea right about now. When a hefty spark lands on the table right in front of me and catches on the stars and stripes placemat, my graceful arm cocks and fires, sending a hail of forks, knives, glasses and lamp chop bones flying across the patio. No one takes note of this, nor do they notice the fire that's started in the dried scrub of the hedge maze. The chromatic fusillade intensifies, the pop-crack is now a deafening salvo of rapid fire explosions directly overhead, and the rain of cinder and ash begins to fall with a fury. One of the Washingtons frantically pats his smoldering wig as I try to size up my options, but the barrage of sight and sound is overloading my senses, and the best I can do is cover my head and hope the assault will pass soon. A rocket, rather than bursting in the air, bursts onto the tennis court next to the stage, and the band suspends its musical accompaniment and scatters for cover along with most of the partiers, although some applaud thinking it was part of the show. When a second rocket slams into the pool house and a third takes out the buffet table, the party's merry mood turns to chaos and pandemonium, and fleeing becomes the predominant activity. No one is clapping now. Now they're running and screaming and tearing off their wigs. Women are tripping over their dresses and no one stops to help. Another fireball lands directly in the midst of the panicked mob, enveloping the terrified guests in a splash of multicolored flames. I scan the landscape for the source of the attack. There, in the farthest corner of the yard behind the rose garden, the rocket launcher; and manning the device I spot a singular figure, a red blotch, madly gesturing. Insufficiently dispatched by Dog, Otto has decided to finally make an appearance at his party, although not as gracious host. The fireworks machine under his control is now spewing its whistling missiles in all directions except atmospherically. The house itself is his principle target and his aim his quite good. Several of the rockets have no trouble finding windows to penetrate, and in no time flames are shooting from the house everywhere, upstairs and down. A ghastly cloud of thick smoke, green, black, and orange fills the patio. It's time to take the dogs and go. But where? Passage through the house is impossible. The only way out for us now is around the increment and across the back path. From there we should be able to make it to the gate. Under the table both dogs are lying at my feet, and not a little concerned. Do something, they are surely telling me. I pull my chair away and Dog emerges without hesitation. But the little dog is paralyzed with fear. It lies pressed against the ground trembling, unable to bring its gaze upward to meet mine. I take the little thing and wrap it in my arms, I can feel its hot breath through my shirt. We set out, Dog measuring his pace to my anxious, halting gait as we locate the walkway through the acrid smoke and whizzing shower of rainbow sparks. When we turn the corner to the increment it is obvious our escape plan would have to be altered. The structure has taken a direct hit and is engulfed in flames. I avert my eyes to a ghastly sight. The raw lumber proves perfect tinder for this kind of ordnance, and it is not completely vacated—the upper floor, where the women made the meals and the children dangled their legs over the side. The survivors stand by just beyond the gruesome flames wailing and screaming, beset with all manner of lamentations, the men are off to one side coughing violently, overcome with smoke. They catch sight of me and cry out, but there's no hearing anything above the horrific commotion. Their desperate gesturing is perfectly clear however: Why this, they say? No more of this. At that moment

I am possessed with a singular notion. I must stop Otto. Somehow, I must get to him and wrest control of his terrible device. I survey the area behind the roses. The machine continues to spit out its rockets at a furious pace, but Otto has disappeared. Then, the hysterical herd of guests part as if a mighty wedge were driven into their midst, and I spot him. He has commandeered the lawn mower from my shack and is heading full bore through the crowd toward the patio. I backtrack down the walkway. Dog is reluctant to follow, while the little one presses all the more closely against me. The mower begins to bounce and jostle as it encounters the deeply creviced patio stones, and Otto, a bloody, shredded figure, is hollering his nonsense and waving his hand madly, furiously for the world to see. When he reaches the edge he makes no effort to stop. The short wall is no match for the speeding mower. Otto and his ride burst right through, over the edge and down the cliff. None would bother to look over the side to view the remains of his preposterous conclusion. None would stop to say that glory's captain gave his last full measure of anything.

Commotion is the title of the story I tell myself about life with the man and the woman, the history of us, syndromatically unavailable to me in its details but always there, underneath, intuitively understood. It doesn't matter that I haven't been able to remember who we used to be or how we came to be here on the side of a mountain in a house built entirely of stone. Why? is the question I should have been asking all along. And now, as I confront not just my own survival but the survival of these dogs, most innocent in all of this, I am suddenly confronted by that one faculty I have always held in such low regard. Like a seizure, not of body, but of the innermost sanctum of memory writhing to expel the darkest of its hold, the tv screen is on once more and I can see now what has barricaded the past from my vision. I was there. Rockets were pouring down on us from all sides, exploding in blinding flashes and terrific cracks, black clouds of smoke burning my eyes, the awful smell of gunpowder choking me, and everywhere people were screaming, pleading for me to do something but I couldn't understand their words, and there were children, in flames running, little bodies incinerated, bodies torn apart and I couldn't move, I was so scared, I wanted to cry out too, stop, no more, but the words stuck in my throat and I tried to run but my legs, there was nothing, the rockets kept falling and I grabbed for something to hold on to but there was nothing, nothing but dirt, I was clutching at dirt for the love of...

Dog lets out a sharp bark. Yes, yes. We need to go. My eyes are full of tears, but there's no time to contemplate memory's cataclysms. I must save these dogs. The way out is blocked now for sure, the house is ablaze, the smoke is too dense to navigate the narrow path. The mass of people are huddled on the tennis court, trapped I think, for the brittle trees are catching, and if the flames don't get them the smoke surely will. Then it comes to me. Behind the wall. If we can make it past the pool and down the secret trail to my private spot...but we must hurry. I gauge the strength in my legs. My first steps are questionable. I don't know if I can do this. I might lose my balance and fall in the pool. I'm not sure if I know how to swim. A sharp pulse shoots through me, an electric surge from spine to ankle, and for a second I believe the tremor is upon me. But rather than collapsing as I am sure I must, I increase my pace, and by the time we make it around the pool, I am running, running like a madman with Dog a step behind barking for all he's worth. We are obliged to leap over those who have stumbled, exhausted, overcome with heat or smoke or too much wine. A pitiful sight, to be sure, but there's no slowing down now. We reach the passageway behind the pool motor and slip behind the wall and take to the trail. The ruts and bumps well known to the wheels of my chair are now treacherous hazards beneath my feet, and it is Dog who confidently navigates our way. I stay close behind and soon we are at the corner of the wall, the place I often came to enjoy a moment's peace. But this place will prove no sanctuary for us. Smoke is rising up from the canyon and blanketing even this remote location. I look out over the edge of the precipice to see that the fire has jumped the cliff and is pouring like a river to the houses below. We won't be able to breathe if we stay here much longer. I turn the corner of the wall and begin to ascend the mountain.

There is no trail for us, no path of flat square stone filled with weeds to lead us on this upward trek. There is only the rough, rock strewn, scraggly desert, nearly too steep to gain a proper foothold. But on this dark night the fire below and the continuing fireworks display lights the way and we press on. When the path becomes uncertain Dog takes over and I follow his surefooted lead. My legs are strong and sure of their capacity. No need to reach out to rock or bramble branch to gain my balance. I hold tight to the frightened little creature in my arms. Dog stops momentarily and lets go a bark, a clear, mighty howl like a trumpet blast into the night. I take the lead again. Follow me, I gesture, and for once a gesture seems strangely inadequate. I feel something else, a fundamental thing, pressing and stirring deep in some abandoned cavern inside me. A sensation so foreign and unexpected I hardly know what to make of it lest I stop and contemplate its significance. But there can be no stopping until we reach the safety of the mountain top. I turn to see how far we've come. The canyon is engulfed in flames, the house of stone and the houses below, down the winding road to the village itself—all of it a roaring conflagration beneath an acrid veil of rainbow colored smoke and ash, the crack and sizzle of missiles from Otto's mad machine spewing in every direction like shooting stars, the percussive thump of their report echoing off the mountain into outer space, the black night obliterated by the kaleidoscopic cataclysm.

And then...there, at the end of road beyond the driveway gates, bounding up the side of the mountainside toward us, the most incredible sight: a parade...of dogs...dogs! Too many to count, beasts of every size and shape, barking like madmen, coming to join us.

Yes, yes, you glorious wonders! You angelic heroes! Here. Hurry. Up here! Up the mountain with me! I've waited so long. Run, run, you beauties. Yes, Dog, you see them too. You knew they would come, didn't you? They heard your great, un-divine voice calling out to them, join us, you cried. I'll show you the way, you told them. Again I feel a stirring in my chest, powerful and urgent, pushing into my throat, a great primal force seeking release, and I can no longer contain it nor would I. As I take the mountain's summit I turn to witness the world I know, perhaps the only one I've ever known, consumed in its own desperate, preposterous conclusion, and I yell, I yell madly, gloriously, for all I am worth ... *NICE VIEW* ! for this goddamn world to hear.

Well, that was something different. It felt tremendously good. You have no idea, Dog, how good that felt. Dog is giving me a quizzical look. He never heard me bark before. The little one tells me he's ready to join the others and I release him from my arms and set him down among the canine multitude that is gathering about me, a veritable host of eager, wagging tails and magnificent noses. Now I turn my gaze westward to the other side of the mountain. And there, beyond, unbeknownst to me, never imagined or conjured in a dream, an ocean of lights, a great metropolis spread out as far as the eye can see. That's where I'll go. I've got something I want to tell them. *Come on, everybody,* I say, and as all my dogs scurry past, I begin my descent.

ACKNOWLEDGMENTS

My sole entry for this page shall be to my very good friend Gregory Hill who by dint of talent and good will has made the construction of this book possible. I am most grateful for his exceptional editorial skills and judgment which I lack in abundance. Moreover, Gregory is the writer I long to be myself and it by his example that I contemplate pressing on when my natural proclivities and native torpor insist a cessation to any further artistic efforts.

Made in the USA
Monee, IL
19 September 2020